RETURN OF THE BOUNTY HUNTER

Ben Daley returns to Alderton after an absence of five years. He hopes to join his family and lead a peaceful life, but his past soon catches up with him. The Collins gang seeks revenge for Ben's activities as a bounty hunter and an attractive young lady, Miss Weller, is caught up in this web of killing. She wishes to return to her family in Boston, but is forced to stay by the events that transpire. Will Ben's skill as a bounty hunter help to save him, or will the final shoot-out decide whether he has collected his last bounty?

RETURN OF THE
BOUNTY HUNTER

Return Of The Bounty Hunter

by

Ron Watkins

Dales Large Print Books
Long Preston, North Yorkshire,
BD23 4ND, England.

British Library Cataloguing in

Watkins, Ron
    Return of the bounty h

    A catalogue record of t
    available from the Brit

    ISBN   978-1-84262-714-3 pbk

First published in Great Britain in 2008 by Robert Hale Limited

Copyright © Ron Watkins 2008

Cover illustration © Gordon Crabb by arrangement with
Alison Eldred

Published in Large Print 2010 by arrangement with
Robert Hale Ltd.

Dales Large Print is an imprint of Library Magna Books Ltd.

Printed and bound in Great Britain by
T.J. (International) Ltd., Cornwall, PL28 8RW

CHAPTER 1

Ben approached the farm warily. He held his horse's reins loosely in his hands as he rode towards it. He was poised at any moment to go for his guns. To all appearances the farm was deserted, but he hadn't lived for over thirty years without being wary of obvious appearances. In fact it was his ability to spot danger a split second before it materialized which had helped him to survive in many tricky situations during those years.

He glanced at his horse. The roan mare had been with him now for the past eight years, and she, too, had the ability to react to danger. She would prick up her ears – a sure sign that she had picked up something with her keen hearing that the human ear couldn't identify. So far the mare's ears had stayed down. It was a good sign.

That was what you did in situations like this – you looked for signs. You kept glancing from right to left in case there was a sudden unexpected movement. Some things you ignored – such as the hens that were scuttling away as your horse approached.

You accepted the physical discomfort. The sweat on your brow was just an inconvenience. He had learned years ago that to try and brush it away with the back of your hand could be the last movement you would make, as the action would leave you exposed to the sudden bullet that could come winging your way.

He was now only about a hundred yards from the farmhouse. There was still no sign of movement. There should be somebody around. A farm was a living entity. Somebody should be busy doing the usual chores that a farm demanded. There was wood to be chopped. Cattle to be milked. Fences to be mended. Water to be carried from the well. There were dozens of jobs to be attended to. But not today. Not on his brother's farm. The silence seemed to mock him as he rode up the last few yards.

He pulled up his horse. He sat still in the saddle before dismounting. His ears still couldn't pick up any sounds. He glanced at the mare. She, too, wasn't showing any signs that there was anybody about.

Ben's gaze was fixed on the front door. It was half open. It seemed to be inviting him to go inside. He wasn't afraid to do it, was he? He had conquered fear in dozens of other tricky situations during his wanderings. He had managed to survive them. Partly, he believed, due to some sixth sense that had come to his aid on several occasions. But now that sixth sense had deserted him. In fact it seemed to be mocking him. It seemed to be saying: 'Get down from your horse and push open the front door.'

He hadn't been to the farm for how long? Three years? Four years? Was it as long as that? Anyhow the door looked much the same as when he had come here last. In fact everything looked the same. Except that there was nobody to greet him. If there was somebody inside the *clink* of his spurs should have warned them of his approach. If they hadn't heard that then the noise the hens made in escaping from under the feet of his mare would have told them that a stranger was approaching.

Well, not exactly a stranger. There was a time when he had come to the farm as a regular visitor. He had sat down to many a meal cooked by his brother's wife, Martha. They had all been excellent meals. Not only had the main course been extremely tasty, but the pudding afterwards, which usually consisted of a fruit pie, would be of the mouth-watering variety. Yes, Martha was an excellent cook.

Why did he think 'was'? Surely nothing had happened to the two of them? Well, three actually, since young Simon would be growing up now. He gave one last glance around. Nothing moved. Even the hens had stopped their incessant clucking and seemed to be waiting for him to get down from his horse.

He took a deep breath and slid from his horse. As his feet touched the ground there came a familiar sound that he had been half-expecting. It was the *click* of a gun. It was followed by the expected request.

'Drop your gun belt, mister.'

CHAPTER 2

Ben complied with the command. There was nothing else he could do at the moment. The person who had obviously stepped out from behind the log-pile would have his gun trained on him. All he could do was to wait and see what would develop.

'Can I turn round?' he demanded.

'I suppose so.' Was there a little uncertainty in the gunman's voice? If so it was something worth his storing in his mind. It was the little things in situations like this that sometimes could be used in his favour. They could give him that important element of breathing space. Which, in turn could be the difference between life and death.

He swung round. Facing him was not a gunman as he had expected, but a youth. Suddenly recognition struck.

'You're young Simon.'

'Who are you?' This time there was even more uncertainty in the youth's voice.

'I'll tell you who he is.' This time it came from another voice. A woman's. 'He's your uncle Ben.'

'Is that true?'

'Of course it is.' The owner of the woman's voice stepped out through the front door. 'He hasn't been here for five years. That's how you can't remember him.'

Simon lowered his gun.

'Thanks,' said Ben, drily.

Martha stood in the doorway. Her face was hard. 'There's only one thing I've got to say to you, Ben. You're not welcome here.'

'Ma, how can you say that?' demanded a shocked Simon.

'How can I say that? Easily. He left Alderton five years ago and hasn't been back here since.'

'Never mind about me,' said Ben. 'Where's Amos?'

For a few moments Martha didn't reply.

When at last she did so, Ben gasped as he took in her statement.

'He's dead. He was shot by two gunmen.'

'He was killed yesterday,' said Simon. 'We've only just finished burying him.'

This time there was even a longer silence. After some moments Ben said: 'What happened?'

'Two men rode up to the farm yesterday. Amos was out here chopping wood. Simon was out the back – at the well, drawing water. I was in the kitchen. Neither of us heard what words passed between them. But we both heard the next sound – the shot. When I rushed out, Amos was dying. The men were galloping away.' She said it in matter-of-fact tones but Ben could sense the hurt that was behind her words.

'I'm sorry,' said Ben, with massive inadequacy.

'Before Dad died he said one word,' said Simon. 'Well it wasn't a word, it was a name.'

'He gave you the name of the killer?' demanded Ben, eagerly.

'He said one word. Sula. Then he died.'

'Sula is a town about nine miles away.'

'I know,' said Ben. 'I've been there.'

'I suppose you want to pay your respects before you go.' The hardness had come back into Martha's voice.

'You'd better show me the grave.' Ben addressed the remark to Simon.

He was led to the back of the farm. A freshly dug piece of land about six feet long testified that it was Amos's last resting-place. Further evidence was the carved wooden cross that stood at its head.

'I'll carve his name and dates later,' said Simon.

Martha indicated to Simon to move away and leave Ben by the grave by himself.

Ben began to speak quietly.

'As you know, Amos, I was never very strong on religion. But I'm offering this prayer to whoever is listening up there. You've been a good man, a good husband and father. You never deserved to die. But that's the way things are. There's only one thing I can promise you now. That I will hunt down the two men who killed you. I'll get them if it takes the rest of my life. I hope that that will make you rest more peacefully, Amos.'

It was obvious that Ben had finished his speech. Simon went to step forward but Martha held his arm to prevent him.

Eventually, Ben walked back towards them. Martha said: 'That was a nice speech, Ben.' She spoke in more conciliatory tones than she had used before.

'Do you think you'll be able to find Dad's killers?' demanded Simon. 'The sheriff came here and he didn't seem to think that there was much chance of finding them.'

'If anyone can find them it's Ben,' stated Martha. 'He's a bounty hunter.'

CHAPTER 3

An hour or so later the three were sitting down to a meal. Martha's hostility towards Ben had thawed after his speech at her husband's graveside. As a result she had invited Ben to stay for a meal.

'It's the first proper meal we've had for two days,' she confessed.

'What did the sheriff say when he came here?' Ben asked.

'Not a lot,' replied Martha. 'He said that the two men probably had a grudge against Amos. That more than likely they weren't local men.'

'That's rubbish,' said Simon, hotly. 'Dad never offended anybody. Nobody could have had a grudge against him.'

'Is the sheriff the same guy who became sheriff when I left the post?' demanded Ben.

'That's him. His name's Callaghan. I'd never trust him to find Amos's killers. He couldn't find a runt pig in a pigsty.'

'You were the sheriff here?' demanded a surprised Simon.

'Yes, Ben used to be the town sheriff,' said Martha. 'That's why we came here. Ben found your father this farm. You were only about nine at the time. For a few years everything was fine.'

'Yes, I remember now,' said Simon, excitedly. 'You're the one who used to visit us. You used to pretend to shoot me. I'd hide under the table and pretend to shoot you back.'

'Yes, that was me,' said Ben, pushing his empty plate away from him.

'I'm afraid I can't offer you any pudding,' said Martha. 'I haven't been in the mood for cooking lately.'

'That's all right,' said Ben. 'The steak was lovely.'

'If you were the sheriff, why did you leave?' demanded Simon.

'Simon! That's Ben's business,' said his

mother, sharply.

Ben sighed. 'I suppose I might as well tell you.'

Martha went to the stove to make the coffee while Ben rolled a cigarette. Simon waited expectantly.

'When I came to Alderton, I was a bounty hunter,' Ben began. 'I'd shot a couple of guys and I came here to claim the bounty reward. It was a few hundred dollars. Well, these guys were part of a gang and so the rest of the gang – there were four of them – came after me.'

'Did you shoot them, too?' demanded Simon, eagerly.

'Eventually. First of all I was shot myself and I almost died. A young lady nursed me back to health.' Ben's recounting of past events had been delivered in even tones but now there was unmistakable emotion in his voice. 'I went after the bounty hunters who had tried to kill me. It took me months, but eventually I caught up with them.'

Ben paused. Simon, who was obviously

bursting with excitement to hear the end of the story, nevertheless managed to keep silent until Ben was ready to begin again.

'In fact they came after me. They knew that the only way it was going to be settled was by a gunfight. This took place in the church.'

'In Alderton?' asked a surprised Simon.

'That's right. When you next go to church look up at the window above the altar. You'll find three or four bullet holes. They came from the fight I had with the outlaws.'

'Gosh,' said Simon. 'So you killed the four of them in a gunfight in the church.'

'I didn't kill them all by myself. There was a preacher – she was a lady preacher – she shot one of the outlaws.'

Again Ben paused. He stared at the fire in the hearth. The two listeners waited for him to finish his story. It seemed ages before he continued. At last he said, 'While I had been away the young lady who had nursed me back to health after I'd been shot had died. She died of tuberculosis. I wasn't here to look after her the same way she had looked after me.'

The hurt in his voice was so apparent that Martha stood up and went over to him. She put her hand on his shoulder.

'You weren't to know, Ben,' she said, softly.

Simon began tactfully to clear away the dishes. Martha waited until he had cleared the table, then said. 'You'll stay the night, Ben?' It was an invitation that she wouldn't have dreamed of offering an hour or so earlier.

Ben hesitated before replying. Simon waited eagerly for his reply.

'I'd be pleased to do so, Martha,' he stated.

CHAPTER 4

The following morning Ben rode into town. He arrived at the sheriff's office before it was open. In order to wait for it to open he went into the coffee house opposite.

While he sat drinking his coffee he looked idly out through the window. He was watching the door of the sheriff's office and so was only half-aware of somebody standing nearby. When he did glance up he saw an attractive young lady in her twenties.

'Excuse me,' she said. 'But do you mind if I sit at the seat opposite?'

Ben had chosen the window seat and there was a spare seat opposite his.

'Not at all,' he replied.

She smiled and took the vacant seat.

'I hope you didn't mind me asking,' she said, after the waitress had taken her order.

'Not at all,' Ben replied. 'Oh, I've said that already, haven't I?'

She smiled again. She really was an attractive young thing, Ben decided. Well, probably not all that young. But everybody under thirty seemed young to him now, he decided ruefully.

'I'm waiting for the sheriff's office to open,' she explained. 'If I sit here I can see when he opens his office.'

Ben was about to ignore the remark, but there was something about the open candour of her face that forced him to give a guarded reply.

'You're waiting for Sheriff Callaghan?'

'That's right. Do you know him?'

'I used to.'

'What sort of man is he to deal with? I mean, is he a straightforward person, or is he devious? I'm sorry,' she added, apologetically. 'I shouldn't be asking you these questions.'

'It's all right. I used to know Callaghan several years ago. I haven't seen him recently, so I can't really answer your questions.' He could have told her that his sister-in-law thought that Callaghan couldn't find a runt pig in a pigsty, but she seemed so eager for reassurance that he felt that he couldn't disillusion her about Callaghan at that moment. Given time she would probably find out for herself that he was not only lazy but about as trustworthy as a cornered rattlesnake.

'I'm a newcomer in town,' she said, as if that explained everything.

Ben turned his attention to finishing his coffee. It was obvious that he intended the conversation to close. There was no point in continuing it. On impulse he looked up from his coffee to her face. It still had the same expression of trusting openness. It reminded him of a young lady he had known several years ago. She was pretty, like the person opposite. And she had trusted him. What had his reaction been? His reaction had been to leave her. He knew he could have stayed. There was no need to go after the rest of the outlaws. At least they would have had a few months' happiness together before she died.

He was aware that the lady opposite had asked him a question.

'The question was would you happen to know the name of a lawyer in town?'

It was a straightforward question. He could have easily answered it. In fact there were two lawyers he could have recommended. He was fairly sure that at least one of them was still in business. Why then did he reply?

'I'm sorry but I've been away for a few years.'

That was the moment when he spotted Callaghan opening his office. With a curt nod in the direction of the young lady he stood and headed out through the door.

A couple of minutes later he was seated in what had once been a familiar office. Callaghan caught him glancing around.

'I suppose you still wish you were sitting in this chair,' he sneered.

Callaghan was about the same age as himself. In his mid thirties. But whereas he didn't carry any extra weight, Callaghan was several stone overweight. He had the red face of a regular whiskey-drinker and this, together with his paunch, flat face and receding hairline added up to a not particularly attractive sheriff.

If Callaghan thought he was going to rile him, then he could think again.

'I've come about my brother's killing,' Ben said, evenly.

'You're a couple of days late. He died two days ago.'

'What did you find out about his killers?'

Callaghan leaned back in his chair which groaned under his weight.

'Normally that is classified information, as you know. But seeing that you are related to the dead man and seeing that you used to sit in this chair yourself...' the sneer had come back into his voice, 'I can tell you that the two men who killed him came from out of town.'

Ben digested the information for a few seconds before asking.

'How can you be so sure?'

'One was riding a black mare. The other

was riding a piebald. They called in at the blacksmith's because the piebald had a shoe loose. The blacksmith fixed it, then they rode off.'

'To kill my brother,' said Ben, tightly.

'That's what it looks like. Your nephew saw them riding away from the farm. He described the same horses.'

'Why should two strangers ride into town and kill my brother?' said Ben, half to himself.

'That's for you to find out,' said Callaghan. 'They obviously came into town and then rode off. They're outsiders. They're not my problem. You were the bounty hunter. You find them.'

'I'll find them,' said Ben.

Callaghan stared at him. Although he disliked the ex-sheriff sitting opposite he had to admit that there was something in Ben's hard tones that signified that he would find them, even if he had to go through hell and high water to do so.

Ben stepped outside the office. He paused

for a moment to take a deep breath of air. There was something corrupt about the office he had just come from. It was nothing positive that anybody could put their finger on, but it stemmed from Callaghan's obvious dislike of him. In the short while that he had known the sheriff before handing over the reins of office to him, his opinion of him had been that he would be a worthless, lazy sheriff. His opinion hadn't changed.

At that moment somebody called his name. 'Daley!'

It was a man on the opposite sidewalk. He wasn't just an ordinary person who was out for a stroll. He was in the act of drawing his gun.

Ben's reaction was instinctive and his movement was like lightning. Although the gunman had half-drawn his gun before Ben's had cleared his holster, the reports of the two guns sounded as one.

CHAPTER 5

Simon could tell his mother was worried by the number of times she kept going to the front porch to scan the track that led to the house. At last he said:

'Uncle Ben has been away a long time.'

'Maybe he had some unfinished business to attend to in town,' she said, brushing her hair from her eyes in a familiar gesture. Although she was on the wrong side of forty she was still an attractive woman. Even in her black widow's clothes she looked smart. The fact was not lost on Simon who had wondered on several occasions during the past days whether she would marry again. He knew he was being a traitor to his father to even think about the prospect. But his father had always brought him up to face facts, and not try to hide from them. The inescapable fact was that his father was dead and that soon they would have to consider how they could run the farm without him.

His mother went to the front porch once more.

'He's bound to be back for dinner, isn't he?' asked Simon.

His stomach told him that it would soon be dinner-time. He knew that his mother had killed a chicken in order to prepare a special meal for his uncle. To kill a chicken was not a decision to be taken lightly. The couple of dozen hens that squawked around the farm were part of its lifeblood. They not only provided them with eggs, which were a standard part of their diet, but also meant that his mother could go into town once a week to sell the surplus eggs in the market.

'You'd better milk the cows,' said his mother. 'If Ben isn't here by then we'll start dinner without him.'

Ben in fact was waiting to be released from prison. A few hours ago he had been congratulating himself on still being quick

enough on the draw to have killed the gunman on the opposite sidewalk. The sounds of
the gunfire had brought people from the
shops on either side of the street. They had
seen a corpse lying on the sidewalk with
blood seeping from a bullet in his heart.

It also brought Callaghan out from the
sheriff's office. His practised eye took in the
situation at once.

'You shot him?' he asked Ben.

'He was drawing on me before I went for
my gun,' stated Ben.

'We'll soon find out the truth,' said Callaghan.

The arrival of the sheriff brought about
the quick dispersal of the crowd. Even if
some of them had witnessed the shooting
most of them were unwilling to support the
unpopular sheriff by helping him to work
out the exact sequence of events that led to
the killing.

The fact that the crowd dispersed quickly
was not lost on Ben.

'I'll have to find somebody who saw that

the gunman drew on me first,' he stated.

'You'll leave that to me. That's my job,' said Callaghan, bristling with importance.

Ben had been languishing in the prison all day. The place itself had a familiar air to him. He had been responsible for putting dozens of prisoners behind its bars when he had been sheriff. The cell in which he had been placed had obviously been unoccupied for some time judging by the dust on the bars. Ben knew that anybody occupying a prison cell would head towards the bars at some time. The prisoner would then grasp the bars as though trying to keep in touch with the outside world. But to Ben's jaundiced gaze the dust on the bars hadn't been touched by human hand.

He wondered how much longer Callaghan was going to take before he released him. He didn't doubt that Callaghan would keep him in prison as long as he could. There was no love lost between them and Callaghan would derive considerable satisfaction out of keeping him in the cell as long as possible.

The one consolation was that Callaghan hadn't taken anything from him except his gun. When examined it gave confirmation that only one shot had been fired. Ben's other personal belongings, such as his wallet and his tobacco were still in his jacket. It meant that he smoked several more cigarettes during the day than he normally would have, but it helped him to pass the time.

His other means of whiling away the time was by trying to guess where he had seen the guy he had shot. He had called his name, 'Daley'. He had obviously been waiting for him. Which added up to a premeditated killing. Or rather an attempted premeditated killing, since he was alive and the gunman was dead.

Ben tried to conjure up in his mind the man's face. He had a beard. But he might have grown that during the past few months. So it was probable that he knew the man when he didn't have a beard. In which case he really had nothing to go on. He hadn't had a good look at the man. Only a glimpse of a figure with a gun in his hand. A gun which he was about to raise and try to send Ben to meet his maker.

When he had been a bounty hunter Ben had made dozens of enemies. Some of them had been tried and hanged and so couldn't have been responsible for trying to shoot him a few hours earlier. On the other hand many of them were members of some gang or other. The gangs tended to consist largely of gunmen who were related – either brothers, or cousins, or uncles. In which case he could have been responsible for getting one member of a family being hanged, and now another of the same family had tried to gain revenge for it. But without success.

Of course the gunman had made a mistake. In the first place he hadn't taken aim with his gun before calling Ben's name. If he had Ben wouldn't now be in the cell smoking another cigarette. The other mistake was in calling Ben's name. This had been a warning that Ben couldn't ignore. So the gunman had in fact made two mistakes. Which suggested that he was not an experienced gunman. If he had been he would have made sure that he had covered Ben with his gun before calling out his name.

There was a familiar sound outside. It was that of somebody walking along the corridor. It was Styles, the deputy sheriff. He was an unattractive character who had become deputy sheriff while Ben was away.

'I've had orders to release you,' said Styles, putting the command he had received into action.

'About time,' said Ben, putting on his jacket.

'The boss had to wait until a witness came forward to confirm your story,' said Styles, defensively.

'I don't suppose there's any point in asking who it was?'

Styles led Ben into the rear office where he handed him his gun belt.

'I wasn't here when the sheriff interviewed her.'

'So it was a woman,' said Ben, as he automatically checked his revolver.

'That didn't take much working out, did it?' sneered Styles.

For the second time that day Ben was happy to leave the sheriff's office. This time he instinctively glanced across at the sidewalk opposite. There was nobody standing there with a gun which was already half-drawn.

A quarter of an hour later he rode up the path towards his brother's farm. Simon greeted him with a huge smile. Martha's greeting was rather cooler.

'You're just in time to carve the chicken,' she informed him.

CHAPTER 6

In Sula, which was to the south of Alderton, a heated discussion was taking place in the Last Sunset saloon. There were six men involved.

A casual glance would have identified them as drifters, the kind of flotsam that was to be found in most states, not only in Texas. If Ben had seen them he would certainly have been able to put names to three of them. They were Collins, Ashton and Gates. He would have unhesitatingly identified them since he had put them behind bars for five years, and they had only recently been released.

The other three, Lane, Trinder and Menzies he wouldn't have recognized. They had become new members of what was known as the Collins gang.

'We should never have let Wilkes go on his

own to try to kill Daley,' said Gates.

'We didn't know that he'd gone to Alderton,' Collins pointed out. 'He didn't tell any of us.'

'It was only when I called to see what happened to him that his landlady told me where he'd gone,' said Gates. 'When I got to Alderton, I was too late. Daley had shot him.'

'He should have known he would never have stood a chance against Daley,' said Collins. 'Daley has killed more men than Wilkes has had hot dinners.'

'He can't have killed all that many,' protested Lane.

'Don't you believe it,' replied Collins. 'He was a bounty hunter before he became sheriff of Alderton. Then he became a bounty hunter again. Then he joined the Texas Rangers. They spent most of their time killing Mexicans, or Apaches.'

'So where does that leave us?' demanded Gates. 'We killed Daley's brother because we had to. But we never figured that Daley himself would return. And now he's killed one of us.'

'It's no good keeping on about it,' said Collins, who was beginning to lose his temper. 'The last thing that Daley can do is to connect Wilkes with us. So we can carry on with our original plan.'

'We'll have to tell Mr Rawlinson about Daley,' stated Trinder.

'I don't see why,' said Collins, sharply.

'You've told him that we've got rid of Daley's brother Amos?'

'Yes. I went to see him yesterday,' said Collins. 'He gave me this.' He held up a bundle of notes.

The faces of the six, which had been downcast until now, all brightened at the sight of the dollar notes.

'How much is there?' demanded Lane.

'One hundred and forty dollars. At the time he thought it was going to be shared out between seven of us. But of course now there are only six.'

'That's twenty-three dollars each,' said Gates.

'Wait a minute,' said Trinder. 'Me and Ashton killed Daley's brother. 'We should have more than the rest of you.'

'That's right,' said Ashton, who was generally silent when the gang were discussing something. But now that he was directly involved he voiced his opinion. 'After all, we were the ones who had to take a chance by killing him.'

Collins sensed that there was going to be an argument. He quickly defused it. 'Mr Rawlinson thought that there would be twenty dollars each for us. So that's what we'll have. Except that you two–' he nodded towards Trinder and Ashton – 'will share Wilkes's money between you. You'll have an extra ten dollars each.'

There was silence for a few moments while the five digested the way he had suggested sharing the money. Their faces showed that they had accepted the arrangement.

'Right, this should keep us for the next few weeks,' said Collins, as he began to share out the dollar bills. 'Until Mr Rawlinson tells us who he wants us to kill next.'

The grins on the faces of the gang told Collins that he wouldn't have any problem in keeping the gang in order for the near future.

CHAPTER 7

For the next few days Ben busied himself around the farm. As he had observed when he rode up to it a week ago, there was quite a lot of work to be done. He had a more than willing helper in Simon. He was always at hand to carry the stakes to strengthen the fencing and then to hold them while Ben hit them into the ground.

Apart from being pleased to have Simon's help, which meant that the tasks were being completed in about half the time it would have taken him if he had been on his own, he was also relieved that Simon didn't seem to be dwelling on the loss of his father. True, whenever they went to the back of the farm to work, Simon always glanced at his father's grave. For a few minutes his face would change from its normal pleasant expression to one of sadness. However he would soon shrug off the feeling and become Ben's normal willing helper.

Simon would work all through the day without complaining until his mother called them in for dinner. The only demand he made was that he wanted Ben to teach him how to shoot. At first Ben was uncertain about the request.

'How old are you, Simon?' he asked.

'Seventeen.'

'You seem to be able to use a gun, since you had me covered with a rifle when I arrived here.'

'It was bluff,' said Simon, with a grin. 'If you'd gone for your revolver I wouldn't have had the nerve to pull the trigger.'

'But you can shoot a bit?'

'Oh, yes. I've killed jack rabbits and prairie chickens. But that's about all.'

Ben stared into the distance while he gathered his thoughts. It certainly made sense for a young man to be able to use a gun. The West was still a lawless place, as the fact that Simon's father had been shot by two gunmen proved. He himself had started using a gun when he was younger than Simon. In fact he had been fourteen at the time. Simon was waiting eagerly for Ben's reply.

'Have you got a revolver?'

'Yes. Dad had two. And a belt.'

'Right. After dinner tonight; there's still a couple of hours of daylight left. I'll give you your first lesson.'

Simon's wide grin told him that he was delighted to hear the answer to his request.

After dinner Simon went into the sitting room to fetch his father's gun belt which was hanging there. He put on the belt. Ben, who had followed him into the room said: 'It fits you.'

Simon produced a pair of guns from a drawer and slid them into the holsters. He found a tin of bullets and began to load them into the guns.

They passed through the kitchen on the way out of the house. Martha looked up from washing up the dishes. She took in the fact that Simon was wearing a pair of guns. Ben half-expected her to make a comment but when it came it wasn't quite what he expected.

'Teach him to shoot straight so that if the bastards who shot Amos ever come back he can shoot them.'

'You don't mind him learning to shoot?'

'Mind? I'd love to be a man so that I could learn to shoot myself.'

Having had the approval of his mother Simon went out eagerly to have his first shooting lesson. They fixed up half a dozen tins on the fence and Ben paced out twenty steps.

'Right,' said Ben. 'They're your targets. Don't rush drawing your revolver. I'll count up to three to make sure that you take it steady. When I say "One", you put your hand on the revolver. When I say "Two" you draw. Then on "Three" you fire.'

Simon did as Ben ordered. But on his first attempt, although he fired six shots at the

45

target, he didn't hit one. He couldn't conceal his disappointment.

'It's all right,' said Ben. 'You've got to get used to the weight of the revolver. Aim a couple of inches above the tins this time.'

Simon followed Ben's advice. This time he managed to hit one of the tins.

'There. You're improving,' said Ben.

About half an hour later, when Martha came out to see how he was progressing, he was able to hit at least two tins every time he tried.

'I'm afraid you've come at the end of the practice,' said Ben.

'Why? There's enough daylight left, isn't there?' demanded Martha.

'Yes, there's enough daylight, but we haven't got enough bullets. We've almost run out of them.'

'Oh, well never mind. We'll have to get some more.'

'I'm going into town tomorrow. I'll get some,' said Ben.

'We've still got a few left,' said Simon.

'Will you show me how you can shoot, Uncle Ben?'

Ben glanced at Martha. She was obviously expecting him to agree with the request.

Ben took up his position on the same spot where Simon had been standing. His right hand moved so quickly that the gun almost seemed to jump into it. Six shots rang out, almost sounding like one – they were so close together. He dented every one of the tins.

'That was great shooting,' said Simon enthusiastically.

It brought a smile to Martha's face.

'As long as you're here, Ben, we'll feel safe.'

CHAPTER 8

The following day Ben rode into Alderton. He knew his first call was going to be an unpleasant one, but he also knew he had no choice – he had to make it. He called at the sheriff's office.

Callaghan was seated behind his desk. Ben sat in the empty seat reserved for visitors although Callaghan hadn't asked him to sit down. Ben observed the tightening around the sheriff's mouth at the fact that he had sat down without being invited.

'Well, what can I do for you?' snapped the sheriff.

'I was wondering whether you had any more information about my brother's killers.'

'No,' was the short reply.

'What about the blacksmith who fixed the shoe of one of the horses? Didn't he give a description of the men?'

'The guy who was on the black horse kept out of sight, so there was no way he could have identified him. The other one was a Mex. As the blacksmith said, they all look the same.' The sheriff smiled mirthlessly.

'A Mex.' There was surprise in Ben's voice.

'Which was one of the reasons why I assumed they came from out of town,' said the sheriff with more than a little self-satisfaction in his voice.

'You could have told me this before,' snapped Ben.

'As you know, we haven't many Mexicans in town, even though we're only thirty miles from the border.'

'What about the guy I killed?'

'We haven't been able to identify him either. He had nothing on him except a few dollar bills.'

'I suppose you've checked him against the rogue's gallery.' Ben was referring to the dozens of Wanted posters that covered the walls of the sheriff's office.

'Are you telling me how to do my job?' snapped the sheriff. He produced a stick of chewing tobacco and began to cut a piece off. Ben rightly assumed that it was time for him to leave.

His next call was the blacksmith who had fixed the horse's shoe. The blacksmith's name was Joe and he greeted Ben with a grin.

'I heard you were back in town, Ben.'

'You heard about my shoot-out?'

'It was the best item of news for the past few days.'

'Yeah, I know. Nothing much seems to happen in Alderton.' How many times had he heard that expression while he was sheriff?

'How can I help you?' demanded Joe.

'I'm checking up on the guy whose horse needed a shoe when they came into town and killed my brother.'

'Yeah, I'm sorry about that. Everybody liked Amos. He was a hard-working farmer.'

'Somebody didn't like him.'

'I see what you mean. That's why he was shot?'

'It certainly looks that way.'

'Well I'm afraid I can't help you with your enquiries. There were two guys who called here. As I told the sheriff, the one kept out of sight. The other one, who was riding the piebald, was a Mex. I don't think I'd recognize him if I saw him again.'

'Was he tall, or short? Did he have a moustache?'

'He was shortish. No, he didn't have a moustache. Wait a minute, the other guy who was waiting outside did say something to the Mex.'

'What did he say?'

'He said, wait here ... then he mentioned the guy's name.'

'Can you remember what it was?'

The blacksmith wrinkled his brow. Reluctantly, he said, 'I'm sorry. I can't remember.'

Ben tried unsuccessfully to conceal his disappointment.

'It will come to me though,' said the blacksmith, reassuringly. 'These things often come to me when I'm busy. Maybe by the time you call next I'll have remembered.'

Ben left the blacksmith's intending to collect his own horse which was tethered at the back of the sheriff's office. When he reached the sheriff's office he changed his mind and crossed the road to the coffee shop. He automatically glanced across the road before doing so. Ben, you're getting ultra cautious he told himself as he entered the shop.

The small room was full and he was about to turn away when a woman waved to him from a table by the window. He hesitated before crossing over to her. It was the same young lady he had seen when he had visited the café on the day before he had had the shoot-out.

'There's an empty seat here,' she said, pointing to the seat opposite.

'Thanks,' said Ben, accepting the seat.

'We'll have to stop meeting like this or people will begin to talk,' she said, with a smile.

Not only a pretty young lady but one with

a sense of humour too, Ben noted as he ordered coffee.

'By the way,' she said, when the waitress had left. 'My name is Carole Weller.' She held out her hand.

Ben took her hand. 'My name is–'

'Ben Daley. Yes, I found out after I saw you shoot that man.'

'You saw the gunfight?'

'Yes. If you remember I intended going over to the sheriff's office. But you left here first and I saw that you went in. So I waited for you to come out. Then, when you did come out, I saw it all. He was already drawing his gun before you started to draw yours. I must say it was great shooting.'

'Thank you,' said a slightly embarrassed Ben.

'When I went over to the sheriff's office I told him that I had seen the whole thing and that the other man started the gunfight.'

'You told the sheriff?'

'Yes. I felt that it was my duty as a citizen.'

'When did you tell him that?'

'Oh, I don't know. About half an hour after the shooting. I stayed here to order another cup of coffee. I waited until they had removed the body, then I went over to the sheriff's office and told the sheriff what I had seen.'

'The bastard!' Ben couldn't contain himself.

'I don't understand.' She gazed at him quizzically.

'I'm sorry for swearing in front of a lady,' he said, contritely.

'It's all right,' she said, smiling. 'I've got two brothers and you'd be surprised at the words they come out with.'

'Perhaps I'd better explain. The sheriff kept me in jail all day for shooting the guy. He said nobody had come forward until then to state that the gunman was drawing his gun before I fired.'

'But I saw it. I told him,' she stated indignantly.

'Well anyhow, I'd like to thank you for telling the sheriff what you saw. If you hadn't

I'd probably be in jail now.'

'You don't like the sheriff,' she observed, as she stirred her coffee thoughtfully.

'You saw him. Are you surprised that we didn't see eye to eye?'

'Not really.' She turned her attention to the window. In a few minutes she swung back again. 'I'm sorry to appear rude, but somebody is supposed to be coming here to meet me.'

'In that case I'd better make myself scarce,' said Ben, finishing his coffee.

'No, please don't go.' She put her hand on his to restrain him. 'I think I'll want some advice.'

'If I can help you...'

She took a deep breath. She had obviously come to a decision. 'I own a small ranch a few miles out of town. It's situated near the road to Sula. That's why I'm here – to see about selling it.'

'That's why you asked about seeing a lawyer when we were talking the last time we met?'

'That's right. As you know, there were two lawyers in town. One of them has closed down. I found this out from the sheriff when I called to see him. Anyhow, I called to see the other lawyer. But he wasn't in his office. He had some business in Sula and he wouldn't be back until today. I've just been to see him and he saw the copy of my grandfather's will. He said it was all in order and that I could go over to the ranch. It was all mine.'

'Congratulations on becoming a landowner,' said Ben.

'Oh, it's no great size. It's only about fifty acres.'

'A fifty-acre ranch when you sell it should get a tidy sum of money,' said Ben.

'The trouble is I haven't been to see it yet.'

'I see – no, I don't. You've been in town a few days–'

'Five to be exact.'

'You could have gone to see it at any time. How far out of town is it?'

'About four miles. I had to wait until the

lawyer confirmed that it was mine. Now I've got another problem. How do I get out there?'

'Pony and trap. You can hire one from the livery stable.'

'You don't understand, do you? All the conversations at the hotel have been about how dangerous the town has suddenly become. There have been two killings in the past week. It's not the sort of place where a young woman should set off on her own to a strange ranch.'

'I see,' said Ben, thoughtfully.

'The lawyer said he'd send somebody round here to ride out with me, but there's no sign of anybody.'

Ben stared at her frank open face. He half-wished it wasn't a face that kept reminding him of another young woman. One whom he'd let down when she had depended on him to help her. He could have easily stayed and helped her. Perhaps she could have recovered from her tuberculosis. They had set up places called retreats in the mountains where they were sent for a cure. He had heard that in some cases it worked.

She was staring at him with a puzzled expression.

'I'll take you out to your ranch,' he heard himself say.

CHAPTER 9

Ben was surprised to find that Carole was a good horsewoman – in fact she was a very good rider indeed. They rode side by side along the deserted road in the direction of Sula. After a while Ben spurred his horse to a quick trot. Carole did the same. Ben's next move was to ride his horse at a quicker pace. Soon they were galloping.

He glanced across at his companion. Her fair hair was blowing in the breeze. She was smiling. Somehow she looked more like a schoolgirl than a young woman. Well, not too young. How old was she? Probably in her late twenties. Still, everybody these days seemed to be young to him. He smiled at her infectious expression of happiness.

'How far did you say the ranch is?' he asked as their horses raced stride for stride.

'About four miles. I haven't been here for years. But I'll know it when we come to it.'

They still had the road to themselves. Ben knew that apart from the occasional buggy or wagon they would be unlikely to come across any signs of life on it. Of course there was the stage – but that only came from Sula twice a week. Today wasn't scheduled for one of its journeys to Alderton. Then there was the occasional rider who, like themselves, would take advantage of the empty road. But so far they hadn't seen anybody.

'We shouldn't be far from there now,' said Carole about ten minutes later.

She had inherited a fifty-acre ranch but she obviously intended to sell it. She didn't intend staying in Alderton. Not that he could blame her. It wasn't exactly a booming town. Other towns not too far away had overtaken it in the development race. Take Sula, for instance; that had been a backwater just like Alderton a few years back. Then the railroad had arrived and everything had changed.

Ben's thoughts were interrupted by Carole's shout.

'It's the ranch. It's on fire.'

She spurred her horse forward and Ben followed suit. They were galloping at full speed towards the tell-tale glow in the sky, which had become a deeper red as they approached.

They swung round a bend and Ben was able to see that the fire had taken over all the ranch. Flames were licking up the side walls, but the fiercest part of the fire was in the roof, which was burning merrily. The flames, mingled with the swirling smoke, meant that Ben didn't get a clear view of the ranch as he galloped towards it. His gaze took in the fact that the ranch had obviously been deserted, since there was no sign of any livestock.

The answer to Ben's unspoken question about who or what had started the fire was revealed when they were about a hundred yards away. The smoke cleared from the place where the corral had been. He was able to see two horsemen who were watching the blaze.

They were so intent on the blaze that they hadn't noticed the approach of the two riders. When they did spot Ben and Carole they automatically went for their guns. Ben's reaction was instinctive. He swept Carole off her horse and dived down to the ground beside her. The sounds of two shots whistling overhead told him that he had been just in time.

'The bastards are shooting at us,' screamed Carole.

Ben didn't have time to notice her choice of epithet. He had drawn his own gun.

'Why don't you shoot back?' she demanded.

Ben knew that he wouldn't have a chance of a good shot at that range. He was waiting for the right opportunity and ignored her remark.

The two men fired a few more shots at Ben and Carole, but since they were lying on the ground they presented difficult targets. The swirling smoke, too, was making their aim more difficult.

The horsemen decided that they would have to change their tactics. They swung their horses round so that they were facing the two figures on the ground.

'What are they going to do now?' demanded Carole.

Ben put his arm around her. 'Don't move,' he whispered.

Ben knew he could take one of the riders. But which one? His first task was to protect Carole. The riders began to move slowly forward.

Were they going to ride one on either side of them? His own tactic depended on the answer to that question.

The two riders separated when they were halfway towards them. It meant that Ben's decision was made for him. He leaned across Carole's body so that he was shielding her from the gunman who was on her side. Then he waited for an opportune moment.

He didn't have to wait long. When the riders were about fifty yards away he took careful aim and fired.

Testimony to the accuracy of his shot was seen by the way the rider toppled from his saddle. Ben instantly swung round to meet the second oncoming rider. However a repeat performance wasn't necessary. The rider, seeing the fate of his companion, swung his horse round in a tight turn and rode like the wind away from the scene.

'You could have tried to shoot him as well,' announced Carole, as she rose to her feet.

'I don't believe in shooting somebody in the back,' retorted Ben.

'Are you going after him?'

'He's got too much of a start.' Ben didn't add that he didn't want to leave her on her own.

They both stared at the house which had rapidly burnt to a shell. The thick corner posts were still standing but the walls had almost completely disappeared. As they watched the remaining part of the roof fell to the ground sending up a shower of sparks. The smoke rose in a grey blanket. The heat from the burning timber reached them as they stood side by side.

Ben glanced at Carole. To his surprise tears were running down her cheeks.

'I'm not normally a cry-baby,' she sobbed.

'It's all right,' replied Ben.

'It's just that I've spent so many happy days here.'

Ben's reaction was instinctive. He put his arms around her. He held her while she sobbed. When she finished crying Ben handed her a handkerchief.

'I'm all right now,' she said, drying her eyes.

CHAPTER 10

When Ben returned to the farm Martha took in his appearance with a frown of disapproval.

'You've been standing too close to a fire,' she said, wrinkling her nose.

'You can say that again,' said Ben, as he took off his jacket.

'So there was a fire?' Martha probed.

'Yes. A big fire.'

Simon entered the room.

'You smell as though you were in the middle of it, Uncle Ben.'

'I can see I'm not going to have any peace until I satisfy your curiosity,' said Ben.

He explained about Carole Weller and their ride out to her ranch. He told them about the fire and how they had been attacked by two gunmen. He concluded by describing how he had managed to kill one of the gunmen.

'You've killed another of the gang,' said Simon, excitedly.

'I'm not exactly sure whether there is any connection with the guy I killed outside the sheriff's office and these two killers,' stated Ben.

'It seems a bit of a coincidence though, doesn't it,' said Martha. 'Two killings in a few days. And in this peaceful town.'

'Yes, there could be a connection, I suppose,' admitted Ben.

'Have you been to see the sheriff?'

'I had to report the killing, although it's outside the sheriff's territory. He's only responsible for what happens in the town.'

'Which means he's not doing anything,' said Martha, flatly.

'You've guessed it,' said Ben, drily.

'This ... Carole Weller ... how did you meet her?' asked Martha, casually. The superficial casualness didn't deceive Ben. He knew her question concealed a keen interest in his answer.

'She was one of the witnesses who saw the guy who tried to kill me outside the sheriff's office. She told the sheriff that he had drawn first. But the sheriff kept me in jail for most of the day, even though he knew I wasn't guilty of murder.'

'You don't like the sheriff, do you, Uncle Ben?' demanded Simon.

'That's the understatement of the year,' stated Ben. 'Anyhow, I was forgetting something important,' he added. He produced a large package. 'There are enough bullets in this to keep you busy for quite a few days.'

Simon accepted the package eagerly. While Simon was concentrating on his shooting practice, Ben divested himself of most of his clothes and proceeded to wash himself thoroughly in water that he drew from the well. Martha brought out a towel for him. She observed that he had a fine body, although there were several scars on it – presumably evidence of old gunfights. She wondered whether the emotional scar left behind by his ex-girlfriend would be too strong to allow him ever to make a commitment to a woman again.

Carole, too was thinking about Ben. She knew she would be eternally grateful to him for saving her life. There was no doubt in her mind that if she had turned up at the ranch on her own and discovered the two men setting fire to it, there would have been only one conclusion. Her life would have ended shortly afterwards. The way the two gunmen had tried to kill them both was evidence about the fact that they held life cheaply. They would probably have killed her and tossed her body on to the fire. She shivered at the thought, even though the afternoon sun was hot.

Why should anybody want to burn her ranch? It wasn't as though there was anything to steal there. It had been empty for months – ever since her grandfather had died. It didn't make sense to burn it to the ground.

She had returned her horse to the livery stable after riding back to town. It was only a short distance to her hotel, but she was glad when she arrived there. She almost kept looking over her shoulder to see whether there was any sign of the remaining gunman.

Don't be foolish, she reproached herself irritably. How could the gunman be in town? He had ridden off in the direction of Sula. So he could hardly have swung round and arrived back in Alderton.

Anyhow, Ben had said that the solution to the mystery about the killings lay in Sula. They had ridden back to town in silence after leaving the ranch. In fact there had only been one brief conversation. She had begun it by asking the question why?

Ben didn't need any further elaboration. He knew exactly what she had been referring to. He had told her about his brother's last word. Sula. So it seemed that the answer to the mystery lay there.

In the hotel she ordered a hot bath. It would be lovely to soak away some of the tension in her limbs. Not to mention getting rid of the smell of the smoke.

A quarter of an hour later she was told that her bath was ready. She sank into its delicious warmth. The thought came unbidden that it was lovely to be alive. Especially having been so near death an hour or so ago.

The adventure would be something to regale her friends with when she arrived back in Boston. She would soon be able to tell them how she had been literally within an inch of death, since one of the bullets had come so near her head that she had felt that it had touched her hair. She brushed her hand over her damp hair as though half-expecting to find a trace of the bullet. She smiled at her foolishness.

There was one thing she regretted though. She wouldn't see Ben again. She would be catching the stage tomorrow. She had already booked her seat on it before going to the ranch. She hadn't told Ben about her decision. Not that they had had too much time for any conversation during their visit to the ranch.

Although their acquaintance had been

short, she knew that Ben was that rare breed of mankind – the sort of person on whom you could depend. Especially when you were in trouble. She sank into the bath so that her head was completely immersed. When she emerged she shook the water out of her ears. Yes, she was an expert in dependable men. Or rather the lack of them, since she had been let down by not only one man, but by two.

In the first place there had been Harry Trubshaw. They had been engaged for four years – in fact he had bought her the diamond ring on her twenty-first birthday. He had seemed a pleasant enough companion. They had indulged in the usual pastimes that the people in social life in Boston indulged in. They had gone to the theatre, dancing, and to the races. If Harry had seemed to be spending too much money on backing the horses, she told herself that it wasn't anything to do with her. Harry worked for his father who was a book publisher and so the family seemed fairly wealthy. Then, one evening three years ago Harry had dropped a bombshell. The printing firm was about to be declared bankrupt. In which case he stated, he assumed that their engagement was at an end.

She had cried for several days afterwards. She felt that the only dream she had had was over. She had sent her engagement ring back to Harry. The hurt hadn't been alleviated when she had found out that the main reason for the publishing firm going into bankruptcy was the fact that Harry had gambled away much of its income during the time they had been engaged.

Her second venture into the field of what women fiction writers call love, came almost a year after Harry's exit from her life. This time his name had been Grahame Culpepper. He was a dashing figure of a man. At the social balls which she had once again been persuaded to frequent, he was never short of female companions. He was witty, and, as the English writer Jane Austen would have said, he was a very agreeable person.

The fact that he had chosen her to be his regular companion made her the envy of her friends. She felt that fate, which had been unkind to her, was now once again smiling on her. Their friendship had blossomed and the time came when the inevitable happened – he asked her to marry him. For some reason which she could never really fathom, she refused him. Well, she didn't actually refuse him, but she told him that she would give her answer the following day.

Of course she knew what that answer was going to be. It would be an unreserved yes.

The next day came and with it news that brought her whole world crumbling around her. Grahame Culpepper was already married. The evidence was there in the front page of the *Boston Times* for everybody to see. In fact he had been married twice already.

Oh, yes, she was an expert on unreliable men. Had she met one of the few of the reliable male species in Ben? Well, she'd never know now. The stage was due to start early in the morning.

CHAPTER 11

When Lane rode into the clearing where the rest of the gang were camping the others greeted him warmly. It took them a few seconds to realize that he was in fact on his own.

'Where's Trinder?' demanded Collins as Lane dismounted.

'He's dead.'

'Dead?' The others stared at him in bewilderment.

'Dead? How?' demanded Collins.

'How do you think? He was shot.' There was an unmistakable belligerence in his tone which didn't match his usual placid nature.

'Who shot him?' demanded Collins.

'I don't know his name. I didn't stop to ask him,' snapped Lane. He accepted a towel that Gates had tossed to him. The horse showed unmistakable signs of having being ridden fiercely as Lane began to rub him down.

'How did Trinder get shot? You two were just supposed to burn down a ranch,' persisted Collins.

'We did. We had just finished when a man and a woman rode up. The man killed Trinder. You didn't tell us that there was any danger in burning the ranch down. You said it was just a simple job. Burn the ranch down and then get away. Unfortunately Trinder didn't get away.'

The outlaws stared at Lane. There was no mistaking the emotion in his voice. In fact he had turned his head away from them so that they couldn't see the pain on his face.

'I'm sorry about Trinder,' said Collins. He knew that Lane and Trinder had been close friends. In fact they had been friends for several years – even before the gang was formed.

'Did you get a good look at the guy who killed Trinder?' demanded Menzies.

'We were riding towards him. He was lying on the ground.' Lane had now turned to face them and he recited the sequence of events in even tones. 'He was shielding the girl as we rode towards them. We split up as we came nearer, so that he couldn't take the two of us. Then, when we were about fifty yards away he picked off Sammy. It was a great shot. He got him with the first bullet.'

'What did you do?' demanded Gates.

'What the hell do you think I did?' snarled Lane. 'I turned and rode back here as fast as I could. I wasn't going to argue with a guy who could shoot like that.'

'He didn't follow you?' demanded Collins

'No. I did turn round to check. He was busy comforting the girl.'

'So it must have been her ranch,' said Gates, thoughtfully.

There was a general murmur of agreement. Collins broke into it with his next question. 'What did he look like?'

'I didn't get a good look at him. There was

smoke everywhere. He was clean-shaven. I think he was rather tall.'

'It was Daley,' said Collins, slowly, like somebody who had just arrived at a self-evident conclusion.

'How do you know?' demanded Menzies.

'Let's just say I know,' snapped Collins.

A couple of them shook their heads at his sudden leap of intuition.

'It could have been anybody,' voiced Gates. 'It could have been the woman's boyfriend.'

'I'm telling you it was Daley. To be able to hit a target which was racing towards you – and kill the rider with one shot. There aren't three people in the territory who could do that. I'm telling you it was Daley.'

A couple of the others obviously disagreed with him. But they wisely kept their opinions to themselves.

'What do we do now?' demanded Gates.

'I'll go to see Mr Rawlinson. I'll tell him that we burnt down the ranch as agreed,' said Collins. 'We'll share the money be-tween us as usual.' He glanced at Lane for confirmation of the decision.

'Yes. That's what Sammy would have wanted,' said Lane, to Collins's relief.

CHAPTER 12

There was one task that Carole felt she must perform before finally saying goodbye to Alderton. It was a rather unpleasant one, but she felt that it was her duty to carry it out. She had to visit the sheriff.

She knew that Ben had already called to see him and had given a description of the killer who had made his escape. She felt that she could help to provide a more accurate description.

The sheriff seemed genuinely pleased to see her. If she hadn't known about him keeping Ben in prison for hours when he could have released him she would have accepted his pleasant smile and invitation to sit down at its face value. But there, she just wasn't a very good judge of men. She smiled ruefully at the thought.

'What can I do for Miss Weller?'

'I believe Mr Daley has explained about our visit to my ranch. And how we were attacked by two gunmen.'

'Yes, he called here earlier. Unfortunately there's nothing I can do about it, since it's outside my territory.'

'I've come to see you since I think I might be able to help to identify the man who rode away.'

'You think you know him?' said a surprised sheriff.

'No, but I would recognize him if I saw him again. I've drawn this picture of him.' She produced a charcoal drawing.

The sheriff examined it. 'That's very good. The drawing, I mean.'

'I'm an artist. I draw pictures for a living.'

The sheriff was still examining the man's face. 'I can't say that I've seen him. He certainly hasn't been a prisoner here.'

'Well, anyhow, this might help you to catch him. I take it you didn't know the man Ben killed either?'

'No.' The sheriff shook his head. 'The undertaker has collected the body, but I don't expect any relative will come along to claim it.' He smiled.

Carole stood up. 'Well, I'll leave you to your work.' It was obvious that he didn't have any work since his desk was clear. But the sarcasm was lost on the sheriff.

Carole went across the road to the coffee house. She'd have one last cup of coffee. She sat in her usual seat. She looked out through the window as though half-expecting Ben to appear on the scene. When there was no sign of him she realized that it had just been a wishful fancy. Ben had gone out of her life for ever. He was already a part of an event in her past.

It would have been nice to have met him once again though. He stood for the quality that the two men in her life had lacked – reliability. He was also quite good-looking. It was a wonder there wasn't a Mrs Daley on the horizon. Of course she had heard the story about the love of his life. It had been related to her by one of the ladies in the hotel. It had certainly been a sad episode. She would have thought that possibly he would have recovered from it by now. Maybe he was waiting for the right person to come along again.

Well, one thing was for sure – it wouldn't be her. She would be on her way to Sula in the morning. So it would be goodbye Alderton and goodbye Ben.

In the excitement of the shooting her first thoughts had centered on revenge. But on reflection she had concluded that it was none of her business. The best thing she could do was to leave it to the law.

Ben was in fact giving Simon shooting practice. He was pleased with the progress his pupil had made. Simon was now hitting three cans out of six.

'Your shooting is improving,' Ben informed him. 'Try to aim a fraction lower. You're getting used to the weight of the gun, which means that you can lower your aim.'

Martha came out to watch them.

'Do you think he'll ever be as good as you, Ben?' she asked.

'The main thing is for him to keep on practising.'

'When he can hit six cans I'll open a bottle of wine,' said Martha.

'In that case I'll move the cans closer so that he hit the six,' replied Ben.

Martha smiled. 'I've been saving the bottles of wine for a special occasion. But since you're one of the family again, I'll open one after dinner. It's elderberry wine.'

'If I remember rightly it used to be quite strong.'

'I think I can guarantee that you'll have a thick head in the morning,' she replied, as she turned and headed for the house.

CHAPTER 13

As Martha had prophesied Ben had a thick head in the morning. The result was that he set off for Alderton later than he intended. He passed the stage as it was drawing out of the town. He didn't give it a second glance; if he had he might have seen a person that he recognized occupying the corner seat – Carole.

Ben had two calls to make. Since one of them was more unpleasant he decided to get it over first. He called in the sheriff's office.

To Ben's surprise Callaghan greeted him with a smile. He waved him to the empty chair.

'Sit down, Ben.'

The false warmth of the sheriff's welcome should have warned Ben that there was something unusual in the offing. When the sheriff offered him a cigar, which Ben refused, the false air of *bonhomie* was even more evident. If Ben's head had been in its usual clear condition he would have deduced that there was something behind the sheriff's new-found friendship.

'I suppose you saw the stage leaving?' said the sheriff.

What had the stage got to do with anything?

'Yes,' replied Ben.

'And you knew of course that Miss Weller was on board?'

The surprise on Ben's face told the sheriff that Ben hadn't known. Well, well, well. This was going even better than he had anticipated. He was going to deliver the blow that Miss Weller was leaving town and obviously wouldn't return. Instead he had delivered a body blow in informing Ben that she was on the stage in the first place. Ben hadn't known!

The sheriff almost purred as he played his

next card.

'She told me when she called here yesterday afternoon.'

'I see.'

The surprise was still evident in Ben's tone.

The sheriff revealed his winning hand.

'She left this.' He produced the drawing Carole had made of the outlaw who had escaped from the gunfight at her ranch.

Ben studied it. It was a good drawing. She had unmistakably caught the outlaw's likeness. It was far superior to all the drawings which hung on the walls around the room.

'She said she was a professional artist. But I expect you already knew that.'

The sheriff watched him closely for any signs that the further piece of information was also something new to Ben.

This time, however, Ben managed to keep a blank face.

A few seconds later Ben stepped outside the sheriff's office. He left without giving an acknowledgement before leaving. He had a lot on his mind.

Why hadn't Carole told him that was leaving on the stage to Sula? She had let him make a fool of himself in front of the sheriff whom he hated. He had assumed that she would still be in Alderton – at least for a few days. Possibly until he could find out more about who had burnt down her grandparents' ranch. Instead of which she had left town without telling him.

It all boiled down to one thing. You couldn't trust a woman. You help them in the first place by taking them to see their ranch. Then, in a shootout you prevent them from coming to any harm. Their reaction? To leave town without telling you. No, not only to leave town, but by giving Callaghan the drawing of the outlaw to make sure you make a complete fool of yourself.

It was almost enough to make a person turn to drink. However he resisted the temptation. He hadn't mounted his horse but was walking it along Main Street. A few walkers on the sidewalk acknowledged him as he passed. He raised his hat to the women politely.

A few of the young ones smiled before turning away. He wondered whether they knew about his recent embarrassment. Maybe they knew that a certain young lady – no, a pretty young lady – had upped sticks and left town without as much as a word of farewell. Not that there was anything between them of course. There couldn't be anyone else in that sense since his beloved Emma had died five years ago. But he had assumed that he and Carole were friends. Well, more than friends – good friends. And as such they wouldn't have secrets from one another. Such as leaving town without telling the other. And being a consummate artist without disclosing the fact.

His stroll during which he tasted these bitter thoughts had brought him to the hotel where Carole had been staying. He was about to pass it when a young lady came out, calling his name: 'Mr Daley?'

'Yes?'

He recognized her as one of the parlour-maids.

'I've got a package for you. Miss Weller left it. It would have been delivered to you later today, but since you're here I can give it to you.'

She suited the action to her words by giving him a package.

'Thanks,' said Ben automatically.

He chose a secluded spot under an over-hanging tree. While his horse was busy grazing, he opened the package.

There were two items. The first he had seen before. It was a copy of the drawing Ben had seen in the sheriff's office. The only difference was that whereas there was no signature on the one in the sheriffs office, this one was signed Carole Weller.

The other item was a letter. It stated that Carole was sorry to leave without saying goodbye. That their short acquaintance had meant a lot to her. That she couldn't thank him enough for going with her to the ranch and for saving her life. That she wished she could have stayed longer in Alderton, but that she had booked the stage the day before. That she would sell the ranch as she had intended to do in the first place. She hoped that the drawing she had made of the outlaw would help in a small way to recompense for her hasty departure, and even help to catch the outlaw. She wished him all the best for the future, and if he ever came to Boston to look her up. She gave her address. She signed the letter: with best wishes, Carole.

The parlour-maid who had given him the letter now came out of the hotel wearing a cloak. She was carrying a basket and was obviously on the way to the stores.

'Is everything all right, Mr Daley?' she demanded, seeing that he had opened the package.

'Yes, everything is all right now, thanks,' he replied.

She flashed him a smile as she passed by.

CHAPTER 14

There were twenty-six saloons in Sula, three hotels and five cafés. There were also fifteen stores, three livery stables, three banks and an opera house. In addition there were four churches, three schools and, tucked away in an inconspicuous street, a brothel. Sula was a bustling town, with its population growing year by year.

After receiving the shattering news that another of their gang had been shot by Daley the members of the Collins gang got rid of their disappointment in their own ways. Mostly this consisted of visiting a saloon and getting drunk. The exception was Ashton. In the first place he wasn't a drinking man. And, in the second place he liked to pursue his favourite occupation – watching the stage or train arrive in the town.

Of all the members of the gang Ashton was the least clever. Indeed he was often the butt of jokes from the others. Not that he minded – he had been called names since he first went to school and the teachers had discovered that he was slow-witted. He had got his own back on them by not turning up for their classes – in fact he had soon decided that there was no point in him turning up for school at all. So he had become a regular absentee. Not that it bothered his parents. They already had eight mouths to feed and the few cents a week they had given Ashton to go to school could easily find a more suitable way of being spent and helping to support the family.

So Ashton had become a vagrant, living on the streets, and existing partly by dint of a little begging and slightly more by stealing. It had been an easy progression into a life of more serious crime, as a result of which he had spent several of his twenty-nine years in prison. Now he was a member of the Collins gang, which he felt was an honourable position. Especially since there was little to do, with the exception of an occasional robbery. He was quick in handling a gun and this had increased his usefulness to the gang during the past year or so. In fact he wasn't exactly sure how long he had been in the gang since to arrive at that conclusion would mean the mental strain of counting. And as his teachers had kept reminding him, he wasn't any good at counting.

The afternoon was pleasant, with the heat from the sun giving way to a pleasant gentle breeze. If Ashton had been of a philosophic bent he could have felt that it was an afternoon when it was good to be alive – especially since two of his friends had been killed and were now in Boot Hill. But not being a philosopher he contented himself with watching the travellers descending from the stage. They all looked weary after their journey from Alderton.

The stage was forced to stop some distance away from the hotels. This was because of the number of carriages which cluttered up the main streets. The carriages owed their presence to the fact that there would be an opera later on this evening in the opera house.

Ashton watched as the last passenger stepped down from the stage. She was a pretty young lady. In fact she was a very pretty young lady. Ashton didn't take his eyes off her as one of the attendants picked up her trunk and proceeded to follow her.

Their progress was halted by a shout from the stage driver.

'Miss Weller, you've left your hat box behind'

Miss Weller! Ashton almost gasped with excitement. This was the young lady whose ranch Lane and Trinder had visited. Here she was in Sula. Ashton turned and raced back to the saloon where he knew he would find the rest of the gang.

CHAPTER 15

Mr Rawlinson always preferred to be addressed by his old army rank of colonel. But since the war had been over for more than twenty years he had been forced to bow to convention and accepted the title of Mister.

He had, however, kept one relic of the old days – his army uniform. Every day he would don it. His servant, Rufus, would brush it, and then stand aside respectfully. The colonel, with his buttons gleaming, would step into the dining-room to have his customary dinner. The other difference between that event and any other which might be happening in houses up and down the country was that Mr Rawlinson would toast Robert E. Lee before sitting down to his meal. The dinner would have been prepared by Rufus's wife, Mary – they were the two remaining servants who had been with him since the Civil War had ended.

The South might have lost the war, but he had won a battle recently. He sighed with satisfaction as he reflected on his strategy. In the first place he had heard by chance about the enemy's movements, the enemy being that cursed representation of the North: the Northern Pacific Railway line. Then by dint of covert questioning he had established that the rumour was correct. They intended building a railway line from Sula to Alderton.

The discovery of the plan had caused him more than a little surprise. He had always imagined Alderton to be a quiet backwater which would probably stay that way for ever. However he had been wrong. There was obviously more than a possibility of expansion in Alderton. Which was why the railway company intended connecting it with Sula.

So he put his plan into action. He had bought most of the land between the two towns. In fact 'bought' was too strong a word, since he managed to become the owner of the land merely by registering it in his name. He had paid the nominal registration fee and it had become his.

Of course, all this had been helped by the fact that the land between the two towns was prairie. Nothing grew there except cactus and a few trees. Nobody could graze cattle on it. It was not even suitable for sheep. He managed to become the owner of the land with hardly any problems. Of course he couldn't register it in Sula – that would have set tongues wagging. Why is Mr Rawlinson buying up this land? What is he up to?

So he had gone to Hawkesville to register the land at the land registry office. Hawkesville was far enough away from Sula. Nobody recognized him as the ex-army colonel.

It wasn't exactly true, though, to say that there had been no problems. In fact there had been one – namely the farm just outside Alderton that was owned by Amos Daley. He had sent a message to Daley saying that he wanted to see him. When Daley had arrived he had told him that he wanted to buy his farm. He had offered him a fair price. But the stubborn farmer had refused the offer. In fact he had come a second time to discuss the possibility of buying the farm. This time he had offered Daley an increased sum for it. Again Daley had refused. This had left Rawlinson with no choice. He had invested so much effort and time into the project that there was only one alternative. He had had Daley killed.

Of course it was a pity – but there it was. Daley had stood in his way. He had no other choice but to have him removed from the equation. There was, too, another slight hiccup. There was another farm outside Alderton which he would have to purchase to complete his plan to own all the land the railway would run on. This was less of a problem since the owners had died a few months ago. So all he had to do was to make sure that the farm wasn't sold as a going concern by having it burnt down.

Yes, he could safely say that everything was going according to plan.

CHAPTER 16

Ashton's arrival in the Last Sunset saloon signalled a halt in the game of cards the other members of the gang were playing.

'What's up?' demanded Collins, seeing the look of agitation on Ashton's face.

'I've seen her,' Ashton gasped.

'Who?' demanded Collins.

'Miss Weller. The lady who owned the farm that Trinder and Lane burnt down.'

'How could you have seen her?' demanded Lane, scornfully. 'You don't even know her.'

'Perhaps he's been dreaming about her,' said Menzies.

'Yes, how could you have seen her? You don't even know her,' probed Collins.

'I was watching the stage from Alderton come in. Some people got off. Then this blonde lady got off.'

'There are plenty of blondes around,' put in Lane.

'Yes, but this one was called Miss Weller.'

'How do you know?' demanded Collins.

'She'd left her hatbox on the stage. The driver called out after her. He mentioned her name,' Ashton concluded, triumphantly.

Whereas until then the response to Ashton's claim had been sceptical and even downright disbelieving the attitude of the four changed abruptly on hearing that declaration.

'Are you sure?' demanded Collins.

'Positive,' replied Aston.

The others stared at Collins while he digested the information. Then he exclaimed triumphantly: 'We've got him.'

'Who?' demanded a puzzled Ashton.

'Why, Daley of course,' replied Collins, impatiently.

'You mean we can get to him through Miss Weller?' said Gates.

'That's right. Daley went with her to visit her grandfather's farm. They are obviously close, otherwise he wouldn't have gone with her. We know it's no good going to Alderton to try to gun down Daley. He'd get at least a couple of us before we had a chance to get him. But if we can use Miss Weller as bait he'll come to us. Then we'll have him on our own terms.'

The others digested the reasoning.

'You mean we'll have to kidnap her?' demanded Ashton.

'Exactly.'

'I'll volunteer to look after her,' said Menzies. 'I'm always interested in blondes.'

'You're interested in anything in a skirt,' said Gates.

The laughter of the others told Collins that his idea had been accepted. 'So where is she?' he demanded.

The others focused on Ashton. For a few seconds he was nonplussed by their attention. Then he blurted out: 'I don't know.'

'What do you mean, you don't know?' snapped Collins.

'You mean you didn't follow her?'

demanded Menzies.

'She went down Main Street. She couldn't have gone far. She was carrying a case and a hatbox,' replied Ashton, defensively.

'You fool.' Lane banged his glass on the table to emphasize his point. The others reacted with warning glances at Lane. The last thing they wanted to do was to attract attention to themselves.

'She couldn't have gone far from the place where the stage drew up,' suggested Ashton, hopefully.

'No, maybe you're right,' said Collins, thoughtfully. 'It's obvious she's staying the night at one of the hotels. The first thing tomorrow we'll start going round them until we find her.'

'I wonder what she's doing in Sula?' put in Menzies.

'I think it's obvious,' said Lane. 'We burnt down the ranch. So there's no reason for her to stay in Alderton.'

'You could be right,' said Collins, thoughtfully. 'Well, whatever the reason we'll start going round the hotels early tomorrow. So finish your drinks and we'll head for the camp.'

Normally this would have brought some protest from the others, since there was still plenty of beer in their glasses, but for once there were no complaints. Tomorrow they would capture Miss Weller. She in turn would lead them to Daley. They couldn't wait to catch him, since, as Collins stated, he had been responsible for killing two of them.

CHAPTER 17

The following morning Carole had a leisurely breakfast. She was in no hurry. She would be spending one day in Sula before catching the train on the following day that would take her to Boston. She had one piece of business to settle before leaving the town, but she could leave that until this afternoon.

She idly contemplated her itinerary for the day as she drank her coffee. For a start she would go shopping. It seemed ages since she had indulged in the pleasurable occupation of looking in some shop windows. Of course it had only been for a few days, but the lack of any fashionable shops in Alderton had made the time she had spent there seem longer. If it hadn't been for Ben it would have seemed an interminable time. But his presence had certainly created a diversion.

What did she mean: he had created a diversion? Meeting him was the best thing that had happened to her for years. He was everything she had always imagined her ideal man to be. Physically strong, quite good-looking, maybe a few years older than her, with a sense of humour, unattached... She banged the cup down irritably causing some of the coffee to spill on the table. Why was she thinking of him?

She had resolved to forget about him. There was no way their paths would ever cross again. At the moment they were nine miles apart, since he was in Alderton and she was here in Sula. Then tomorrow, after she had stepped on to the train she would end up a couple of hundred miles away from him. So it was goodbye Ben for ever.

It had been pleasant though on the one occasion when he had held her in his arms after he had killed one of the outlaws who had burnt down her ranch. She would have liked that moment to have gone on. For a split second she had thought he was going to kiss her. He had looked down at her. Their faces had been close. She thought he was going to bring his lips to hers. It seemed the obvious conclusion to their closeness. Just a thank you kiss for saving her life. But suddenly the scene changed. Never again to be repeated, she thought savagely, as she banged her coffee cup down and spilled some more.

An hour or so later she was strolling down Main Street. It was crowded and several times she was forced to step into a shop doorway to avoid a lady who was pushing one of the newfangled perambulators. Why did they have to make them so big? she thought irritably, as she stepped aside once more. One thing was for sure, if she ever had a baby she would never buy one of those ungainly contraptions. What was she thinking about – if she ever had a baby. In the first place she would have to have a man – that was about as likely as her riding in the Kentucky Derby.

She visited several shops. Apart from buying a couple of scarves and some boxes of embroidered handkerchiefs as presents for her friends, she didn't buy much. Indeed the enthusiasm with which she had set out to visit the shops had been tempered, and it largely disappeared as she went down Main Street and then continued looking at the stores along South Street. She eventually entered a coffee house and chose a corner seat.

There was one last task for her to complete before leaving Sula. It was not a particularly pleasant one, but she knew she would have to go ahead with it. She had to visit Mr Rawlinson. He had offered her a price for the ranch. She would have to accept it. Either that, or put the ranch up for auction and go through the whole boring process of selling it to the highest bidder. Anyhow, maybe the price that Mr Rawlinson was going to offer would be higher than she would get in an auction. So if she hung on she could lose out on the deal.

Of course Mr Rawlinson hadn't said how

much he was prepared to pay. He was playing his cards close to his chest. In any
bargaining situation, though, he would find
that she wasn't a pushover. Her father had
been an auctioneer before he had died of
pneumonia when she was a teenager. She
had often visited the auction rooms and
stood in the corner watching the bidders
vying with each other for some property or
furniture or valuables. Yes, Mr Rawlinson
would find that she would be prepared to
get as good a price for the ranch as she
could.

CHAPTER 18

Ben looked at the drawing that Carole had made of the outlaw. Martha caught him taking it out of his wallet and commented: 'There's nothing much you can do about it, Ben, is there?'

'What do you mean?' he demanded, putting the drawing back carefully.

'You know what I mean. She's gone and that's the end of the matter.'

'I wasn't thinking about Carole,' retorted Ben.

'Oh, no.' She laughed scornfully.

'I keep wondering whether I've seen him before. At the time when I was sheriff.'

'You're not a very good liar, Ben,' she replied, ruffling his hair as she passed him.

Ben was seated in the kitchen, having chosen to have a smoke after working in the field through the afternoon. By keeping busy for most of the day he had managed to put Carole out of his mind, but not any longer. Last night he had had this strange dream. In it he had plainly seen Emma, the young woman he had loved and then had deserted. They had been in a large field. He couldn't see clearly what they were doing there. But he could see Emma clearly. She had been wearing a white dress. The strange thing was, she had been walking away from him. And he hadn't followed her. He knew he should have followed her, but she went further and further away. In the end she was just a small figure in the distance. But although she was a long way off he could see her gesture clearly enough. She waved to him, before disappearing completely.

He awoke in a sweat.

What did it mean? Did it mean that Emma was releasing him from his ties with her? He knew that he would carry the guilt of leaving her to die until his own dying day. But maybe in the dream she had been telling him that she was now going out of his life for ever.

Martha stirred his thoughts even more. 'Miss Weller should have told you that she was going to leave Alderton.'

Ben defended her. 'We didn't talk much when we rode back from her farm. She was still upset from seeing it burnt down.'

'That's understandable. But she had time when you were stabling the horse. You must have been at the livery stable for ten minutes or so. She had plenty of time to tell you then.'

Their conversation was interrupted by the arrival of Simon.

'I've done it, Uncle Ben,' he exclaimed, excitedly.

'Done what, Simon?'

'I've hit the target six times. Just like you did.'

Ben smiled. 'Come on then. You'd better show me.'

When they were outside Simon carefully arranged the cans on the wall. He stepped back, counting the paces. When he stopped he announced, 'This is where you stood Uncle Ben, isn't it?'

Ben nodded in agreement.

Simon took a deep breath to steady himself. Then he drew his revolver and fired six times in rapid succession. He hit each tin. Martha, who had been standing in the doorway, clapped her hands.

'That was great,' said Ben.

'Is there anything else I should try?' asked Simon.

'I've taught you everything I know. It's up to you to keep on practising.'

'So that's the end of my lessons,' said Simon, emptying the spent cartridges from the revolver.

'Well, there is one final tip.'

'What's that?' demanded Simon.

'If you're ever in a shoot-out, which God forbid, then this is the tip I received from an old sheriff. He said never stand facing your opponent square on.'

'Like this, you mean?' Simon faced him.

'Yeah. If you're in a one to one fight, turn sideways on to the other guy.' Simon turned as Ben instructed. 'That way if he does manage to put a bullet into you, the chances are it will hit your arm, not one of your vital parts. A busted arm can always be repaired but a bullet in the heart means you're a gonner.'

'I'll remember that, Uncle Ben. I'll practise standing sideways and shooting tomorrow.'

Ben watched Simon as he went into the house. Well, at least Martha should be safe from any attackers now that Simon had learned to shoot. He supposed he had achieved something during his stay at the farm. As for Carole – the only thing to do was to forget about her. For a few wild hours he had forgotten about the vow that he had made to himself that he would always be true to his beloved Emma. Well, since Carole was in Sula and he was here in Alderton it would be easier for him to keep his promise.

CHAPTER 19

At noon the gang met in the Last Sunset saloon as arranged. It was obvious from their expressions that they had all drawn a blank in their efforts to find Miss Weller.

'Sula is a big town,' said Lane.

'She could be anywhere,' said Gates.

'There are plenty of pretty young ladies in the town, but we didn't see Miss Weller,' supplied Menzies.

'Me and Ashton went to most of the hotels which were near the square where the stage-coach pulled up,' said Collins. 'But we couldn't find her.'

'We said we were her cousins,' said Ashton.

'It's a pity you didn't follow her to find out where she was staying,' snapped Gates.

'That's enough,' said Collins, sensing that

trouble was brewing. 'We'll just keep on looking for her. She can't be far away.'

'If she was carrying a suitcase and a hat-box she must be near the square,' said Menzies. 'Otherwise she would have found somebody to carry them for her.'

'That's what I think,' said Collins. 'She's probably in one of the half a dozen hotels near the square. We tried them all, but I bet those behind the desks wouldn't give us the information.'

'Even though we said we were her cousins,' put in Ashton.

'Right, we'll finish these drinks, then we go back to look for her,' said Collins.

Normally the thought of not staying for a few more drinks would have riled the others, but this time they accepted the suggestion without any dissent.

'Do we keep in pairs, or do we split up this time?' demanded Gates.

'You'll have to change your partner. I want Lane to come with me.'

'I'm not having that idiot coming with

me.' Gates pointed to Ashton.

'Then you and Menzies will keep together,' stated Collins.

'Where are we going?' demanded Lane.

'I'm going to see Mr Rawlinson. We haven't been paid yet for burning down the farm.'

'Why are you taking Lane with you?' demanded Gates.

'Because he was the one who helped to burn the farm down. Mr Rawlinson isn't going to hand over the money without asking a few questions. I'll want Lane to be there to answer them.'

They split up as Collins suggested. Ashton and Menzies headed back towards the square where the stage had pulled in. Gates wandered idly down Main Street, while Collins and Lane went to collect their horses.

Menzies and Ashton studied each young woman as they passed them. Menzies gave the pretty ones more than a perfunctory glance.

'You said she was a blonde,' he demanded.

'That's right. A pretty blonde.'

'How did you see her face if she was walking away from you?'

'The stage driver called her name. She turned round to come back to fetch her hatbox,' explained Ashton.

'Oh, yes, I remember you said that. So there's no point in me looking at the dark-haired beauties,' said Menzies, regretfully.

'I wouldn't think so,' agreed Ashton.

Gates, who had chosen to search on his own, was also looking for a blonde. Not that there were many of them around. Sula was only a few miles from the border and many of the ladies were Mexican or of Mexican descent. It meant that they were dark-skinned and dark-haired. So he passed most of them without giving them a second glance.

After walking for about ten minutes he came to the end of what would be termed the smart area. Main Street changed its character. Whereas there had been stores interspersed with houses that stood behind large lawns, there were now wooden shacks which were huddled together. Outside many of them small groups of children, mostly Mexican, were playing. Some of them were begging and tried their luck on Gates. His answer was to ignore them.

He turned round and headed back towards the more civilized side of Sula. He passed the opera house. He wondered idly whether Miss Weller would be going there tonight. He noticed that some famous Italian tenor was performing there in an opera named *Pagliacci*. It meant nothing to him. His knowledge of music was confined to that performed by ladies who regularly sang in the saloons.

He had strolled back almost to his starting point when he was jerked out of his leisurely stroll by the sight of Menzies running towards him. He hurried to meet him.

'We've found her,' gasped Menzies.

'Where is she?' demanded Gates.

'She's heading for the livery stable.'

'Right, come on then.'

The two of them began to run towards the livery stable. When they arrived there Ashton had already collected their horses.

'Where is she?' demanded Gates, in a whisper.

Ashton nodded towards a young lady who was waiting while one of the stable boys hitched up a pony to a buggy. She was standing idly looking into the distance. Menzies pursed his lips in appreciation. She was certainly a good-looking filly herself.

CHAPTER 20

Collins and Lane quickly covered the couple of miles to Mr Rawlinson's house. Collins dismounted by the wrought-iron gate.

'It doesn't look as though he likes visitors,' observed Lane, taking in the long barbed-wire fence that enclosed the grounds.

They went through the gate and Collins closed it after them, in accordance with the notice which adjured: 'Shut the gate'.

An avenue of trees bordered the drive that led up to the house. They let their horses walk up to the house. Through the trees Lane spied a strange circle of bricks. They stood a couple of feet high and obviously enclosed some sort of pit.

'What's that for?' demanded Lane.

'It's a bear pit. Some of these old colonial houses had them. It seems that bear-baiting was very popular in the days before the Civil War.'

'So that's what these old Southern gentlemen did for entertainment.'

'Be careful you don't say anything against the old Southern gentleman. He's the last of the line.'

Collins had half-prepared Lane to meet an unusual character but he almost failed to conceal his surprise when he saw that Mr Rawlinson was wearing his army uniform. They were greeted in the drawing-room by Mr Rawlinson and the servant, Rufus, who stood at a respectable distance behind the colonel.

'Sit down.' The colonel waved them to chairs.

'I've brought Mr Lane with me,' Collins began. 'He was one of my men who burnt the ranch down.'

'Good, good.' Mr Rawlinson rubbed his hands together.

Lane was so interested in the sword that the colonel was wearing that he almost missed the fact that it was his cue to speak. Collins had warned him not to say anything about the appearance of Daley and that Trinder had been killed.

'It went according to plan,' he stated. 'We burnt it down. It was a wooden building and burned easily.'

'Most of the buildings these days are wooden,' stated the colonel. 'This is one of the few stone buildings in the locality.'

'Do we take it that this is the last of our assignments, sir?' demanded Collins.

'I think so. Yes, I think we can safely say this is the end of the line.' The colonel smiled. Rufus's face too split into a smile as though he were sharing a secret with the colonel.

Collins and Lane waited for the colonel to continue.

The colonel gestured to Rufus, who went to a desk. He opened a drawer and produced a large envelope.

'Here's the payment we agreed upon. You may count it if you like.'

'I don't think that will be necessary,' said

Collins, as he accepted the envelope from Rufus.

'There is one other thing,' said the colonel. 'Both of us have been engaged in unlawful activities. It might occur to you at some later stage to try to blackmail me...'

Collins shook his head vigorously.

'Oh, you may deny it now. But at some future time you might see fit to change your mind. If you do you will find the full force of the law against you. I have deposited a letter with my lawyer stating that the shooting of Mr Daley and the burning of the ranch were both entirely your own ideas. That you didn't tell me about the events until after they had happened. That you hoped to receive payments for them. Of course, being a gentleman, I refused.'

The two waited until they were a suitable distance away from the house before Lane vented his feelings.

'The bastard!' he cried.

'He knows how to cover his back,' stated Collins. 'He wasn't a colonel for nothing.'

CHAPTER 21

Carole first became aware that she was being followed when she pulled across to allow the stage to pass. To think that twenty-four hours ago she herself had arrived at Sula on the same stage. And that in another twenty-four hours she would be leaving, not by stage this time, but by train.

As she waited for the stage to pass she glanced idly behind her. At first she didn't think it strange that there were three riders a short distance behind her who had also pulled across to allow the stage to pass. They were the only other riders in sight.

When the stage had passed, on its way to cover the mile or so towards Sula, Carole flicked her whip at the horse. It obeyed the unspoken command and started on its way. The lawyer in Alderton had told her that Mr

Rawlinson lived in a large house a couple of miles outside Sula. She couldn't miss it. It stood a few hundred yards back from the road, but was easily recognizable since it was the only house on that particular stretch of the highway.

Her mind centered on her expected meeting with Mr Rawlinson. No doubt he would assume, since she was a woman, that he could offer her a low price for the ranch and she would accept it. Well, he would certainly be in for a surprise. Although the ranch was isolated and in fact there were no other ranches within several miles, her grandparents had been successful in keeping it going for many years. She didn't know exactly how many, but she guessed it was about twenty. How did they keep a lonely ranch like that going, grazing sheep on it? Even growing corn? The answer was that there was a stream running through the ranch.

As far as she knew it was the only stream running through the land. It started way back in the hills where it was merely a spring. Several years ago her grandfather had taken her up into the hills to show her the spring. She had seen the clear water gushing out of the ground. It never dried up, her grandfather had told her. To her surprise he had knelt down, cupped his hands and, having collected some of the water, proceeded to drink it. After drinking a few times he had invited her to do the same. She had knelt down and, after a couple of false attempts when the water had escaped through her fingers, she had managed to trap enough to drink it. It had been the loveliest drink that she had ever tasted. Pure water, her grandfather had informed her.

So it could be a profitable, working ranch if someone like Mr Rawlinson bought it. She wouldn't be selling a useless piece of land. It was fifty acres of land which contained that precious commodity – water. Not for the first time she wondered why Mr Rawlinson was interested in buying it. The lawyer in Alderton had told her that he was an old man. So she could assume that he didn't want to live there and farm it himself. Especially since he owned a large house here near Sula. Maybe he had relatives, such as a son who would like to run the ranch. Yes, that was a possibility. Of course whoever bought it would have to build a new house. But that wouldn't be too much of a problem. They could knock up these wooden houses in a few days.

As she drove along she scanned the land on her right. It was scrub land without a building in sight. It was only fit for cactus to grow among the tough grass. It was certainly not suitable for grazing. There were some trees here and there which broke up the monotony of the landscape. She should be nearing Mr Rawlinson's house now. What had the lawyer said it was called? Yes, she had it. *La Casa Grande*. Well, she certainly knew enough Spanish to realize that that meant The Big House.

Her reverie was interrupted by the realization that she had arrived at the house. Or rather, the gate that led up to the house, she corrected herself.

She jumped down from the buggy and opened the gate. To her surprise she saw that the three riders whom she had spotted earlier, had also stopped behind her. Maybe they were visiting Mr Rawlinson, too. Well, she was certainly not going to leave the gate open for them. Let them open it themselves, she thought, irritably, as she drove through, jumped down and closed it behind her. It closed with a satisfying clang.

She had driven a short distance along the drive when she realized that her original assumption had been right. The 'clang' of the gate told her that the riders had also come through it.

There was nothing odd in that, she told herself. Mr Rawlinson probably often had visitors. The fact that the three riders had set out from Sula at roughly the same time as she had meant nothing. Nevertheless she felt a shiver of unease as she flicked the whip at the horse to make him go faster.

She was tempted to turn round to see if

the riders were keeping their distance. She managed to resist it. Anyhow she could now see the house in the distance. Another few minutes and she would have arrived safely within its protection.

Mr Rawlinson must be having a busy afternoon, since there were two riders coming towards her. They had obviously just left the house. There wasn't enough room for them to pass her if she carried on along the driveway. It meant that they would have to ride on the grass to pass. Not that it made much difference since there were wide expanses of neatly trimmed grass on either side of the driveway.

As the two riders came nearer a terrible realization struck her. Although the odds must be 1,000–1, she recognized one of them. It was the outlaw who had ridden away after burning down her grandparents' ranch.

Panic seized her. She knew she had to get away from him before he recognized her. She drew up the pony in a cloud of dust. She pulled on the left-hand rein to turn the buggy around. It never completed the man-oeuvre. At the same time as she was trying to turn it a strange object whistled through the air. It landed around her shoulders. It took her a second to realize that she had been lassoed by one of the riders behind her. As she struggled desperately to free herself from the clinging trap she felt herself being pulled out of her seat. She clung to the reins in a desperate attempt to stay on the buggy. The horse, reacting to the sudden tightening of its own reins, reared. Carole was thrown against the iron corner of the buggy. She hit her head against it with some considerable force. The result was that she lost interest in any further proceedings as she blacked out.

CHAPTER 22

'She's passed out,' said Ashton.

'That's obvious,' snapped Collins.

'How does that effect our plan?' demanded Menzies. He had carried the unconscious Carole from the place where she had fallen off the buggy to a more secluded spot under some trees.

'It doesn't,' replied Collins. 'In fact it makes it easier.'

'In what way?' demanded Lane.

'We just send one of us to the ranch where Daley is staying. Whoever it is will be carrying a letter saying that we've got Miss Weller a prisoner. If he wants to see her alive he'd better come and see us.'

'How will Daley know we've got her?' demanded Gates.

'That's easy,' said Collins. He produced a

knife. He took hold of Carole's head and cut off a lock of her hair. He held it up. 'Daley will recognize that this belongs to his girl-friend.'

The smiles on the faces of the others told him that they agreed with his plan.

'Who's going to deliver the letter?' demanded Ashton.

'Gates,' replied Collins.

The smile disappeared from Gates's face. 'Why me?'

'Daley doesn't know you. He knows the rest of us. If he sees one of us ride up to the farm he'll know who we are and go for his guns. If you ride up, you could be a stranger just passing though.'

'Ask for some water, that's always a good reason for riding up to the farm,' advised Menzies.

'All right, I'll go,' said a rather unwilling Gates.

Collins produced a pencil. 'Has anyone got some paper?' he demanded.

Lane produced a notebook. Collins proceeded to write a note in large capitals. He ripped out the page.

'I don't suppose you've got an envelope?'

Lane shook his head.

'I've got one,' said Menzies. 'I was going to send a letter to a friend who's still in prison,' he said, by way of explanation. He handed the envelope to Collins.

Collins wrote on the envelope, put the letter inside and handed it to Gates.

'What did you say in the letter?' demanded Ashton.

'I just said that we've got Goldilocks here, as a prisoner. If he wants to see her alive he'd better come to Mr Rawlinson's house called *La Casa Grande*.'

'What if he goes to the sheriff in Sula before coming here?' demanded Lane.

'He wouldn't do that,' stated Collins. 'He'd know that if he did he would find her dead body.'

'Do you know where the farm is?' demanded Menzies.

'Yes, it's about a mile this side of Alderton.

We talked about it when we were thinking of a few of us turning up there and having a shoot-out with him. Maybe that would be the better plan after all,' suggested Gates, hopefully.

'This is a better idea,' said Collins. 'This way none of us should get hurt.'

The four watched as a reluctant Gates set off.

'How long do you think it will be before he returns?' demanded Ashton.

'Let me see. It should take him a couple of hours to get to the Daleys' farm. Another couple of hours to get back. Say four hours.'

'What do we do with Sleeping Beauty?' demanded Menzies, pointing to the still inert figure of Carole.

'We'll take her further away from this place. We're too near the driveway here. There's a clump of trees in the distance. If anybody else should come to visit Mr Rawlinson, we'll be too far away for them to see us.'

'How do you suggest that we meet Daley?'

demanded Ashton.

'You and me will be hidden near the gate. If by some trick he manages to get past us, Lane and Menzies will be here waiting for him. One way or the other it will be good-bye, Daley.'

'So we'll have to wait for about four hours,' said Lane.

'More or less. We'll move to our new hiding-place.'

Menzies turned to Ashton. 'Will you take my horse? I'll carry Sleeping Beauty.'

The others set off with their horses to their new hiding-place. Menzies followed, carrying Carole in his arms. When the others were out of earshot, he whispered to the unconscious figure.

'I've got plans for you, beauty, when you wake up.'

CHAPTER 23

Carole opened her eyes. It took her a few seconds to focus. When she did she saw two men's faces peering down at her.

'Sleeping Beauty is awake,' said one.

'We haven't gagged you,' said the other. 'If you scream you're too far from the house for anyone to hear you.'

What were they talking about? Who were they?

She put the question into words. 'Who are you?'

'Don't pretend you don't know us,' snapped Lane. 'I'm the one who burnt down your ranch. Your boyfriend shot at me.'

What was he talking about? Why was her mind a blank? Who were the two ruffians who were standing over her? Why were her arms pinned with a lasso?

Lane put his face down to hers. 'You remember me, don't you?'

She hesitated before replying. 'No-o.'

'That bang on the head must have made her lose her memory,' stated Menzies.

'It doesn't make any difference whether she remembers her boyfriend or not. She'll be able to watch him when he dies.'

Who were they talking about? What boyfriend? Why had the Mexican untied the rope around her, and why was he now carrying her in his arms?

She thought about struggling, but her head began to ache again. It would be better to wait and see what was going to happen.

Her curiosity was soon satisfied when they arrived at the site of an ancient form of entertainment which she correctly identi-fied as a bear pit.

'What are you going to do with me?' she cried.

'I'm just going to have some fun,' said Menzies. 'Your boyfriend won't be here for another hour or so. While we're waiting, I've got plans for you.'

Carole's reply was to spit in his face.

'Now that wasn't a very ladylike thing to do,' said Menzies, as he carried her down the steps into the pit. 'If you're going to struggle it should make things more interesting.'

An hour or so earlier Gates had approached the farm where Daley was staying. He had slowed down his horse to a walking pace when he had arrived within a couple of hundred yards of the farm. He knew Daley's deadly record with a gun and he had no desire to become yet another of his victims.

During the couple of hours it had taken him to reach this spot, he had gone over Collins's plan. The more he had thought about, the more ridiculous it had seemed. In the first place there was no guarantee that Daley would do as Collins expected and come riding to rescue Miss Weller. The fact that Daley had gone with her to the Wellers' ranch didn't mean that they were any more than just acquaintances. If that was so then why should Daley ride to Mr Rawlinson's house to try to rescue her? Daley's obvious course of action would be to ride to Sula, tell the sheriff about the fact that the gang was holding Miss Weller prisoner, and then leave it to the sheriff and his deputies to go and rescue her. In which case, of course, there wouldn't be many of the gang left alive if it came to a gunfight between the gang and the sheriff and his men.

No, the more he thought about it, the more stupid Collins's plan became. There was one thing, though. If Daley did alert the sheriff instead of trying to rescue Miss Weller himself, then he, Gates, might be in an advantageous position. For example, he wouldn't be involved in any gunfight on Mr Rawlinson's land. He would be a few miles away. Yes, it could be to his advantage after all, coming here to deliver the message. The main thing to do was to take his time in riding back to join the gang. That way any gunfight would be over before he reached the house.

Yes, things weren't so black after all. He

had been thinking that he was unlucky to have been chosen to deliver the message to Daley. But on second thoughts it could well work out in his favour.

He arrived at the entrance to the farm. There was no gate. Just a dirt drive about a couple of hundred yards long that led up to the house. There was nobody in sight. This was going to be easy after all.

He held the reins loosely while the horse approached the front door. There was a porch with a few pretty purple flowers growing round it. It was the sort of porch where people sat in the evening after a day's work. The fact that it was still only late afternoon might account for the fact that nobody was seated on the porch. Of course, the other alternative might be that there was nobody at home. If so, that exceeded his expectations. All he had to do was to place Collins's letter on the seat in the porch. Then ride off as quickly as he could.

His horse disturbed some chickens who were pecking at something they had found on the driveway. They squawked in protest as they scuttled away. Gates cursed them as he continued his steady progress towards the porch.

His ears were strained for any slight tell-tale sound. He thought he could now distinguish the sound of an axe. He wasn't exactly sure, though. Whatever the muffled sound was it came from the back of the house. Moreover, he was sure that it was a good distance away. If it was Daley then he doubted whether the noise the chickens had made would have alerted him to his approach. Anyhow, after the first couple of squawks the birds had now gone quiet. There were no more on the drive to make any further noise and he was now only about fifty yards away from the door. Another couple of minutes and he would put the letter on the porch and be on his way.

'That's far enough, mister.' The door had opened and a man was standing there with a gun in his hand. Gates automatically reined in his horse.

His first reaction was panic. How was he

going to talk himself out of this situation? Then he realized with growing relief that the person standing in the doorway was only a lad. Probably only about eighteen. So therefore he had nothing to fear. His hand slowly moved towards his revolver.

'Unbuckle your gunbelt and drop it, mister.'

Gates's mind was working like lightning. He was still about thirty yards away from the boy. It was about the end of the range for getting in a telling shot. But he had done it before. On several occasions in fact. There was no way that the boy could shoot accurately at that distance. You had to be a skilled gunfighter to kill in such circumstances.

He ignored the boy's command and let his hand slide towards his gun.

'I said drop your gunbelt, mister.'

This time there was panic in the boy's voice. It suited Gates. It meant that the boy was a scared youth. It was a pity that he would have to kill him, but he had no other choice.

He went for his gun. The boy didn't seem in any hurry to shoot. This split second of hesitancy was in Gates's favour. He had drawn his own revolver and was about to fire when the boy fired.

Gates didn't have time for any more thoughts as Simon's bullet caught him between the eyes.

'What was the shooting?' Ben, who had been at the far end of the ranch, came running round the corner.

'I killed him, Uncle Ben. He was going for his gun.'

Simon seemed quite calm about the event, Ben thought, as he bent down to examine the corpse.

'It was a great shot,' he announced as he searched Gates's pockets.

'Thanks,' Simon replied. 'Ma is gone into town. What will we do with the body?'

Ben ignored Simon's question and was reading Collins's note. His expression changed as he read it.

'What's up, Uncle Ben?' demanded a

puzzled Simon.

'I've got to go to Sula. Throw a blanket over the body. Then, when your mother returns, go into town and tell the sheriff about the body. He'll send a deputy out to sort it out.'

'Do you know who he is?'

'I haven't seen him before, but I bet he is one of the Collins gang.'

Ben was on his way into the house when he called out:

'Saddle my horse for me will you, Simon?' So saying he headed for the kitchen where his gun belt was hanging. He put on the belt, made sure that he had enough bullets and was back out as Simon was finishing saddling the horse.

'This is why I've got to go to Sula.' He handed Simon the note. 'If I don't come back remember that there's a bounty on that outlaw.'

He disappeared down the drive in a cloud of dust.

CHAPTER 24

About half an hour after Ben had left the farm Martha returned. She drove the buggy up the driveway and stopped at the form covered by a blanket.

'What's that?' she demanded.

Simon, who had been sitting on the porch waiting for his mother to return, replied succinctly: 'A body.'

'I guessed as much. But who is it?'

Simon stepped forward and pulled the blanket away. 'His name is Len Gates. I found an old pack of cards in his pocket. His name was written on the outside of the packet.'

'Who killed him? Your uncle Ben?'

'No, I did.' Simon couldn't conceal a hint of pride in his voice.

'You did?'

'Yes, Ma. This is what happened.' Simon explained exactly how Gates had died.

'So where was Ben when this happened?'

'He was at the far end of the ranch. By the time he got here I'd shot Gates.'

'So where is Ben now?'

'He's gone to Sula.' Simon explained about the letter Gates had been going to deliver. Martha went pale on hearing how Ben had rushed off to try to help Miss Weller. Simon was expecting some sort of praise for Ben for his action. Instead Martha said: 'The fool.'

'Why do you say that, Ma?'

'Because he's going to get himself killed, that's why. He's obviously going into a trap. Gates wouldn't have ridden from Sula just to deliver a letter.'

'Maybe Uncle Ben has worked out some way of getting Miss Weller away from the gang without either of them being killed.'

'Let's hope he has.' She changed the subject. 'What are we going to do with him?'

'Uncle Ben told me to report it to the

sheriff. He also said that it was possible there was a bounty for killing Gates.'

'Well, you'd better ride into town to see the sheriff. The sooner he comes to fetch this outlaw the better.'

Simon saddled his horse and rode into town. The sheriff was about to close his office when Simon rode up.

'What is it, Simon?' demanded the sheriff, as he was about to lock the door.

'I've come to report a killing.'

'Don't say your uncle has killed somebody else?' questioned the sheriff with an attempt at humour.

'No, I killed this one.'

The sheriff shot Simon a keen glance. 'I suppose you'd better come into the office and tell me about it.' He pushed open the door and led Simon into the office. When he was seated behind the desk, he began with: 'You'd better tell me exactly what happened.'

Simon explained how Gates had arrived at the farm. He concluded with the description of the way he had killed him. The sheriff couldn't keep the surprise from his voice.

'You killed him with one shot?'

'Yes, Uncle Ben has been teaching me how to shoot while he's been staying with us,' replied Simon with pride.

'I see. I suppose I'd better come out to see the body.' There was more than a hint of annoyance in his voice. He had been looking forward to going to his lodgings where his landlady would have prepared a large evening meal for him. Now he would be at least half an hour late.

'There's just one thing?'

The sheriff stopped in the act of getting out of his chair. 'What's that?'

'Uncle Ben said that there was a good chance that there was bounty money on Len Gates. I'll just look at these drawings before we go.'

'Well, don't take long. I haven't got all day,' snapped the sheriff.

Simon started to search the hundred or so

drawings of outlaws which were on the walls. The sheriff grew more and more impatient. At this rate he would be more than a half-hour late for his meal. More like an hour if the pain in the arse of a boy didn't hurry up. He'd had a bellyful of the Daleys in the past few days. First there was Ben shooting that guy outside the office. Then again there was Ben shooting the outlaw who was setting fire to Miss Weller's farm. The fact that Daley didn't know that she was an artist had given him some moments of satisfaction. But now, on top of it all this boy was going round the walls searching for a picture to match the guy he had shot. All the time his dinner would be getting cold. His landlady would have let the fire go out once she had cooked the dinner. He could guarantee that by the time he arrived at his lodgings his dinner would be completely spoiled. And it was all the fault of the bloody Daleys.

'Here he is!' exclaimed Simon, excitedly.

The sheriff forced his portly form to his feet. He went over to examine the drawing.

It said plainly: Len Gates. Wanted for murder.

'How much bounty will I get for killing him?'

'Three hundred dollars,' snapped a disgruntled sheriff.

'Whew! Uncle Ben will be pleased,' stated a delighted Simon.

CHAPTER 25

Ben was in fact less than a mile from Mr Rawlinson's house. He was galloping towards what he instinctively knew was a trap. The question was, what was he going to do about it when he arrived at the house? Ben, who prided himself on always being honest with himself, only had one answer. He hadn't the faintest idea.

The beat of the horse's hoofs seemed to repeat the question over and over. What are you going to do?

He knew they would be waiting for him. How many? That was a crucial question. If there were only two left in the gang then he reckoned he would have a fifty-fifty chance of getting them before they managed to shoot him. But if there were more than two then he would have no chance.

He remembered the house from the several occasions when he had visited Sula. It was a large white house about a couple of miles this side of Sula. It stood in large grounds with a plantation of trees that helped to obscure the houses from the vision of passers-by, particularly travellers on the stage. To further protect its privacy Mr Rawlinson, or maybe the previous owner, had erected a strong, forbidding barbed-wire fence around it. And he was going to ride up to this fortress and expect that he could rescue Carole. Who did he think he was fooling?

The thought occurred to him, not for the first time, that maybe he should give up the idea of rescuing her. He could ride past the house into Sula. He knew the sheriff there, Paul Thackery. He had called to see him on several occasions when he was hunting some outlaw or other. Paul was a young, energetic, friendly sheriff. He didn't dislike bounty hunters, as did some sheriffs. Paul realized that bounty hunters provided a useful service in hunting outlaws who were outside his territory.

Yes, the thought occurred to him for the umpteenth time that he should leave it to Paul and his two deputies to ride out and rescue Carole. The snag was that if he followed that course he knew with unquestionable certainty that when Paul and his deputies arrived at Mr Rawlinson's house they would inevitably find a dead body. Carole's.

In fact Carole was very much alive. She was fighting, if not for her life, then for her honour.

She had been in the pit with Menzies for about ten minutes and so far had managed to evade him. In the centre of the pit was a thick iron pole to which they used to tie the bears. Carole and Menzies had circled the pole in a macabre dance several times. So far Carole had managed to dodge all of Menzies' attempted lunges and keep out of his reach. But she knew that it was only a matter of time before she became too exhausted to keep evading his clutching hands.

Lane, who was standing near the steps to make sure that she didn't try to escape that way, was shouting encouragement to Menzies.

'That's it! Go on! Get her!'

She had always been nimble on her feet. She was a good dancer and as such had always been in demand at the social balls. Her card had always been full. Many of the beaux had been disappointed that they hadn't managed to have a dance with her. It was this nimbleness on her feet which had so far kept her out of the reach of the lunging Menzies.

Although the midday sun had passed over several hours before, it was still very hot. The heat seemed to be focused on the white wall around the pit. Her clothes were sticking to her and the heat had plastered her hair to her head. Now and again a drop of perspiration ran down her forehead, forcing her to brush it aside impatiently. Menzies grunted with his effort to try to catch her. It gave her some slight satisfaction to know that he, too, was feeling the strain.

'Go on. Get her.' Lane was shouting more encouragement.

She realized with sickening horror that she was losing her concentration when Menzies' grasping hand managed to seize her dress. She instantly pulled away. The result was a distinctive sound of a dress ripping. And an even more distinctive part of her body exposed to Menzies and Lane.

Menzies held aloft in triumph the part of her dress that he managed to rip away. He waved it like a triumphant flag before tossing it to Lane.

She had lost half of her dress and her shoulders were now bare. It was as if the sight of the bare flesh further inflamed Menzies' passion. He chased her with a new-found energy. She stumbled as she tried to evade him. For one sickening moment she though he had caught her. But again it was only a part of her dress that gave way in his grasp.

Menzies tossed it up to Lane. She knew she wouldn't be able to keep up dodging him for much longer. Her legs felt like rubber. She stumbled once more, but this time Menzies wasn't able to take advantage of it. They stood fazing one another. Carole's only protection was the pole that stood in the middle of the pit. She was breathing heavily and as she did so she was aware that Menzies was staring at her breasts – a good part of them was now revealed, since her dress had been torn off. Menzies licked his lips as he stared at her. It didn't take a mind-reader to guess the thoughts that were running through his mind.

Suddenly they both heard it. It was the sound of a shot. It came from the direction of the road. Both stood poised while they waited for any further sounds. Suddenly two more shots came from the same direction.

What did it mean? Carole knew that the other two members of the gang were waiting for Ben to turn up. Did the shots mean that he had ridden into a trap. Oh, no! Her mind reeled at the thought.

Menzies, sensing her hesitation, made another grab at her. She just managed to evade his fingers by a split second. However he was successful in grabbing her petticoat. It ripped from top to bottom as she pulled away from his grasp.

'Hurrah!' shouted Lane, as Menzies tossed the garment to him.

She was now more than half-naked as they began circling round the pole. How much longer could she keep it up? On a couple of occasions Menzies' face had become a blur and little lights were dancing in front of her eyes. Desperate thoughts drummed through her mind. Where was Ben? Had he been killed by the two outlaws who were waiting by the gate? If Ben was dead then what point was there in her keeping on evading Menzies? Why didn't she let him have his way with her and then kill her, too?

Suddenly she stumbled. Menzies seized his chance. He dived at her. She fell to the ground with Menzies on top of her.

CHAPTER 26

Collins and Ashton had spotted the rider when he was still about half a mile away. He was galloping towards them.

'It's him,' said Collins, tersely.

'Do you think he knows we're waiting for him?' demanded Ashton.

'Of course he knows,' snapped Collins. 'He probably thinks he can ride past us and reach Miss Weller before we can get a good shot at him.'

They were both staring fascinated at the approaching horseman. 'He's slowed down,' said Ashton.

'He'll have to pass between us,' said Collins. 'You stand by this pillar. I'll take the other one. Don't shoot until he gets near enough,' he warned, as he took up his position by the other pillar.

In fact Ben hadn't merely slowed down. He had drawn up. He sat in the saddle surveying the gate which was about a hundred yards ahead. There were two sturdy pillars on either side of the gate. They were the sort of pillars that could easily conceal an outlaw. Especially an outlaw who had expected a bounty hunter to ride into a trap.

There was one thing in Ben's favour. No one had shot at him so far. This probably meant that the waiting outlaws didn't possess rifles. If they had they would probably have tried to pick him off when he was at least a hundred yards or so back up the trail. He surveyed the land before deciding on his next move.

What about Carole? Shouldn't he throw caution to the winds? Shouldn't he ride hell-for-leather towards the gate and hope that his sudden burst of movement would put them off their intended shots at him? At least put them off long enough for him to gallop past them and on to the drive leading to Mr Rawlinson's house.

He visualized the scene. Then rejected it almost immediately. If, as he assumed, there were two outlaws stationed behind the pillars his chance of riding between them and escaping unscathed were nil. Anyhow, Carole should be safe until he made his move. The question was, what was that move going to be?

He surveyed the land opposite the house. This was the usual scrub land with the occasional cottonwood tree. Nobody had built a house there. In fact there wasn't another house for the next mile or so – until you started approaching Sula.

Behind the pillar Ashton was getting impatient. Why didn't Daley make his move? He'd been standing there for what seemed like ages. He couldn't tell exactly how many minutes since he didn't carry a watch. Anyhow a watch wouldn't be of any use to him, since he couldn't tell the time.

He glanced across at Collins. He was concentrating fully on the rider and didn't notice Ashton's enquiring glance. Collins had pulled his Stetson down on his forehead to avoid staring straight into the evening sun. Ashton wasn't wearing a hat and so had to endure the sun's rays which silhouetted Daley, making him look like a menacing figure in black on his horse.

Ashton's patience was running out. Also he was feeling uncomfortable since his bladder was full. How far away was Daley? Just about too far to aim accurately with a Colt. Sometimes, though, he had known a revolver shot to kill somebody when it appeared that the person was out of range. The thought persisted and gnawed at his mind.

Ben was considering the possibility of riding on to the prairie to his right. Yes, that seemed to be his best bet. There were a couple of cottonwood trees that would give him some cover. These were situated almost exactly opposite the gate. Yes, that seemed to be his best chance of winging one of the outlaws.

Suddenly a voice erupted from near the

gate. 'What's the matter, Daley? Are you yellow?' It was Ashton. It was followed by a shot. It was a speculative one that died harmlessly on the road.

'You fool!' snarled Collins. He had moved his head slightly forward in his anger. It had been enough for Ben to spot the Stetson. So, just as he had assumed, there were two.

Until then the road had been empty. No rider or horse and cart had passed. But now Ben heard the sound of horses behind him. He turned and a familiar sight met his eyes. It was the stage.

The stage driver was letting the horses gallop. In fact he probably didn't have much choice. The four horses, all regulars on this run, probably realized that they were nearing their destination. In ten minutes' time they would be in Sula. Then there would be welcome water and oats for them. If the driver tried to slow them down he would be met with more than a little resistance.

The passengers on the stage, too, weren't complaining about the unusual increase in speed. The cramped conditions in the stage weren't the best way of travelling. They, too, were looking forward to arriving at their destinations.

Ben drew his horse to one side to allow the stage to pass. Ashton was watching the stage with growing excitement. It had always fascinated him and his one ambition had always been to drive the stage. It was almost level with him when he realized that something was wrong. Was he seeing things? Instead of one person riding shotgun there were now two. Worse than that, one of them was pointing a rifle at him. Ashton grasped the full significance of it, that Daley had jumped up on the stage as it passed him. He tried a shot at Ben, but even as he fired he knew that it was hopeless.

Ben's shot unerringly found his heart.

CHAPTER 27

In Mr Rawlinson's dining room dinner was being served. The ritual for the evening meal was the same every day. Mr Rawlinson would dress for dinner. But not in the traditional dinner jacket and white shirt. Instead he would be impeccably dressed in his old army uniform.

Although the Civil War had been over for twenty years the blue serge uniform was still in excellent condition, thanks to the daily attentions of Rufus and his wife, Mary. Rufus would polish the buttons and Mary would brush it and iron it. Mr Rawlinson even insisted on sitting down to his meal with his sword strapped on. This, too, received loving attention from Rufus, with both the sword and scabbard being polished regularly.

The other concession to tradition was that

Mr Rawlinson sometimes held a musical evening. The only participants were Rufus and Mary. Rufus would play the piano while Mary, who had a pleasant voice, would sing the songs that were part of the tradition of the South. Usually when Mary sang 'Dixie' there would be tears rolling down Mr Rawlinson's face.

While Mr Rawlinson was waiting for Mary to serve the soup he went over the events of the afternoon. It was nice to have finished with those outlaws once and for all. In ordinary circumstances he wouldn't have let them into his house. But needs must when the Devil drives. All he had to do was to wait until Miss Weller came to see him. He would offer her a price for the ranch which was below its value. She might reply that the price was too low. In which case he would pretend to be generous by raising it. Actually he would only be raising it to what he had expected to pay in the first place. She would assume that he was a kind Southern gentleman. Of course he was nothing of the kind.

He was a hard-nosed business man.

Mary brought in the soup.

Yes, he had surprised Collins and his henchman by revealing just how astute a businessman he was. He had noted the surprise on their faces when he had told them he had deposited a letter with his lawyer which would put them away from the rest of their lives. Or even see that they were hanged if they tried to double-cross him.

Normally nothing disturbed his solitary meal. But today it was interrupted by the sounds of a gunshot. He paused in the act of spooning some soup.

'What do you think, Rufus? Was that on our land?'

'It seemed fairly close,' ventured Rufus.

'Yes, it did, didn't it?'

They both waited for further shots. Mr Rawlinson was about to continue drinking his soup when there came the unmistakable sounds of two more shots.

Rufus glanced at his master.

'I'm going to find out what's going on,' he

said, rising from the table.

Carole was struggling like a wild cat. Menzies was lying on top of her, preventing her from getting up. So she had resorted to her only defence. She was clawing and scratching at his face.

He was swearing at her in Spanish as he struggled to get her remaining clothes off. From the top of the steps Lane was shouting encouragement.

After the sounds of the initial shots there had been no more firing. The only sounds came from the pit where Carole screeched as Menzies tugged at one of her remaining garments – her corset. She tried to wriggle out from underneath him, but he was too strong for her.

'I could hit you unconscious,' he hissed. 'But that would take a lot of the pleasure out of what I intend.'

His threat didn't diminish her struggles. His neck was near her face. She stretched forward and bit it.

'Ow!' he yelled. His reaction was to raise his fist. He was on the point of hitting her, when he changed his mind. 'You'll wish you hadn't done that when I've finished with you,' he gritted.

Suddenly he had managed to release her corset. He tossed it up to Lane. Carole was now more scantily dressed than a chorus girl in a cheap stage show.

'I've got you, my beauty,' snarled Menzies as he prepared to take off her remaining garment.

Carole's reaction was to try to cover her breasts which were now exposed. Dimly she realized that Menzies wasn't interested in them. He was fumbling between her legs. She was holding his hand as he was trying to reach his goal. But she was no match for him. His hand had found its goal.

Carole who was still trying vainly to turn over away from his clutching hand suddenly realized that she had one glimmer of hope. He had pulled her own hand away from his objective and she had been forced to put her hand down on the pit floor to steady herself. Her hand was on the layer of dust which had gathered over the years. She didn't hesitate. She grabbed a handful of it and flung it into Menzies' face.

'A-ah!' His howl was partly because he had been instantly blinded and partly out of frustration that he had been so near getting the reward for his endeavours.

Carole struggled to her feet while Menzies dabbed at his eyes to clear his vision. At that moment a strange apparition appeared, riding towards them. It was Mr Rawlinson. He was riding a white horse and in his hand he held, not a gun, but a sword.

'Charge!' he said, holding the sword before him in the time-honoured way of the cavalry.

The three in front of him watched his approach with varying degrees of disbelief. Lane was the first to recover when he realized that Menzies was heading for him. He went for his gun.

Mr Rawlinson was already near enough to

nullify the threat. He did it by the simple expedient of slicing into Lane's throat with his sword. Lane collapsed in a pool of blood.

Mr Rawlinson swung his horse in a tight turn to deal with Menzies. However the Mexican, now instantly alert to the danger, leaped out of the pit. By the time Mr Rawlinson had turned his horse, Menzies had grabbed his gun. The white horse was still a few yards away from him when he shot the rider in the chest. Mr Rawlinson slowly toppled out of the saddle. He had led his last charge.

Carole was still standing in the pit. Was Menzies going to come back in? Were they going to resume their struggle? She stared at him defiantly.

Menzies' answer was to grin wolfishly. 'I couldn't have you. But I'll get your boyfriend. I can promise you that.' He flung the words at her before jumping on to Mr Rawlinson's white horse and galloping away.

Carole gathered up the remnants of her clothes. Her mind was numb after her ordeal.

Suddenly she heard another rider approaching.

Oh, God! Not another one going to attack her?

The rider came in sight and she recognized Ben. A wave of relief engulfed her. He was asking her a question. What was it?

'Who attacked you?'

'It was Menzies.' It was surprising how steady her voice was.

Ben had dismounted and was approaching her. 'Did he...'

'No. Mr Rawlinson came here in time. He shot the other outlaw–'

'Lane.'

'But Menzies shot Mr Rawlinson.'

'Where's Menzies now?'

'He rode off on Mr Rawlinson's horse. Didn't you see him?'

'No, I rode up to the house thinking I would see the other outlaws there. A servant told me in which direction to find you.' He jumped down into the pit. He held out his jacket to cover some of her nakedness.

To his surprise she backed away.

'What's the matter?'

'I'll tell you what's the matter. I never want a man to touch me again. Ever. Do you understand? Not you or any other man.'

CHAPTER 28

Half an hour later Ben was outside the back of the house. He was digging a grave. Rufus had gone into Sula to fetch the sheriff. Carole was watching Ben through the library window.

She was wearing the clothes and frock that Mary had brought her. They fitted her almost perfectly, since they belonged to Mary's daughter. She occasionally came to the house and would stay with them for a while.

Carole was watching Ben, who was stripped to the waist. He was certainly a fine figure of a man. She noticed the tell-tale marks on his body where he had been shot several years ago. Of course she knew the story. How he had had five bullets inside him. How the doctor had managed to take them out to save his life. How his girlfriend had spent months nursing him back to health. Then, when he had recovered he had ridden off to catch the outlaws who had shot him. In the meantime she had contracted TB and died. How Ben had never forgiven himself for not staying with her. Yes, it was a sad story. Not that it meant anything to her now. Especially since she had given up any association with men.

Mary came into the library with two cups of coffee on a tray.

'I must say Louise's dress suits you,' she said, handing Carole one of the cups.

'Yes, we must be about the same size,' replied Carole. 'When I go into Sula and get my own clothes, I'll bring it back.'

'There's no hurry,' said Mary. 'Anyhow, there's something I've got to tell you.' For a moment she seemed too embarrassed to begin. Then she blurted out. 'The colonel was the person behind having your ranch burnt down.'

'The colonel.' Carole was so astonished that she almost spilled some of her coffee.

'Yes. He also paid the outlaws to shoot Mr Daley's brother.'

'Oh, no!' she gasped. This time she did spill some of her coffee.

When she had recovered she asked the obvious question. 'Why?'

'I overheard the conversation he had with the outlaw when he came here the first time. That's how I knew about the plan to burn your ranch. I told Rufus. We couldn't understand why, either. We decided to stay on as his servants. Then if we could find out why he did it, we would report it to the sheriff. I only found out the answer a couple of hours ago when the two outlaws came here.' She paused.

'What is the connection between having Ben's brother shot and burning down my ranch?' demanded Carole.

'They're going to build a railway from Sula to Alderton. Your ranch and Mr Daley's brother's ranch were the only two obstacles in the way.'

'So Mr Rawlinson had Ben's brother shot

and my ranch burnt down so that he could control the land that the railway was going to be built on. I was sorry when he was shot. But now I think he deserved it.'

'We always thought he was eccentric. But by getting mixed up with the outlaws we decided he was mad.'

Shortly afterwards the sheriff arrived with Rufus. They drew up their horses and the sheriff went over to Ben.

'Well, Ben, it's nice to see you again.' He offered his hand.

'I won't shake hands. Mine isn't too clean.'

'What's a bit of dirt among old friends?' They shook hands.

'I assume that grave is for Mr Rawlinson.' The sheriff studied the almost completed grave.

'Yes, he was shot by one of the outlaws.'

'Rufus has been giving me all the details while we were riding back here. There's one thing I don't understand, though. Why did the outlaws want Miss Weller as a bait to get you here?'

Carole, who had joined them, provided the answer.

'They wanted to get even with Ben because he had killed two of their gang.'

The sheriff stared appraisingly as Ben. 'I see you've been busy,' he stated, drily.

'The one guy wanted to get even with me for something that happened in the past. I never even found out what it was. I managed to shoot the other while they were burning down Carole's ranch.'

'There's one other thing you should know, Sheriff,' said Carole. She repeated what Mary had told her about Mr Rawlinson.

'The bastard!' said Ben. 'So he had Amos killed so that he could control the land they were going to build the railway on.'

Carole took in the pain on his face. She would have liked to show by some small gesture that the pain he suffered, she suffered, too. At other times she would have shown her sympathy by going close to him and touching his arm.

But she had forsworn all contact with men.

And after all, Ben was every inch a man.

While the sheriff and Ben were talking about Collins and his gang, Rufus went inside the house. He was met in the library by Mary.

'Is Carole coming back inside?' she asked. 'I'll put some food for her and Ben. And the sheriff, too,' she added.

'I think they're discussing the outlaws,' Rufus replied.

Mary went to the window to watch them.

'You know Carole is in love with Ben,' she stated.

'You've been reading the horoscopes again.' Rufus laughed.

'She was watching him through the window,' his wife retorted.

'So were you, I bet. That doesn't mean to say you are in love with him.'

'I wasn't watching him for twenty minutes,' she replied, in tones that brooked no argument.

CHAPTER 29

Menzies met Collins in the Last Sunset saloon.

'How did you escape from Daley?' demanded Collins.

'After the mad colonel had almost cut off Lane's head with his sword, I was able to shoot him.'

'You shot the colonel?' said Collins, aghast.

'I had to. Otherwise he would probably have cut off my head as well.'

'You know what this means. It means we'll be hunted by every lawman and bounty hunter in the territory.'

'It doesn't matter.' Menzies finished his beer and ordered another.

'What do you mean, it doesn't matter?' snapped Collins.

'I've got it worked out. We slip over the

border tonight. I've got relatives in Limos. We'll be safe there.'

'Don't be stupid. Daley will find us.'

'How can he?'

'You're forgetting that he spent a few years in the Texas Rangers. Where were the Texas Rangers operating?'

'In Mexico,' replied Menzies, slowly.

'Exactly. He's spent more time in Mexico in the last few years than you have. He'll know the governors in the towns. I wouldn't be surprised if he can even speak Spanish.'

'I'd forgotten about that.' Menzies' disappointment showed on his face. 'So what are we going to do? Maybe we can go up North. To Canada. We can escape from Daley that way.'

'There's no escape. They say that the last time he was shot he hunted down the outlaws. He went almost as far as Canada.'

'So he caught them up there?'

'No, they decided to come back to Alderton to shoot it out with Daley. They thought it was their only chance.'

'And Daley shot them?'

'Apparently he had some help from a young lady. Anyhow, that's the story.'

Menzies ordered another beer.

'You haven't told me how you managed to get away from Daley.'

'He was lucky. He knew we were waiting for him. There was no way he could get past us to rescue Miss Weller. The stage happened to be passing. He jumped up on to it. When he passed us he was on top with a rifle. He shot Ashton.'

'What did you do?'

'I didn't have time to get a shot at him. Anyhow, I didn't wait for him to get a shot at me. He had a rifle and I only had a revolver. So I rode off across the prairie. He didn't follow me because he was concentrating on rescuing Miss Weller.'

'Another two minutes and I would have had her at my mercy,' said Menzies regretfully.

'Never mind about that. We've got to plan how we're going to get rid of Daley, once and for all.'

They buried Mr Rawlinson as he would have wished, with a Confederate flag draped over him. The sheriff had gone back into Sula. The four of them sang the hymn: 'We'll all gather at the river'. Mary had a beautiful voice and made its rendering quite tuneful. Afterwards Mary sobbed quietly. Carole put her arms around her.

'It's for the best,' Carole said. 'He was going out of his mind.'

'You're quite right, my dear,' Mary replied. 'But until the last year he was a good man to work for.'

Rufus and Mary wanted Ben and Carole to stay at *La Casa Grande*.

'You'll be safe here,' said Rufus.

'Leave hunting them down to the sheriff and his deputies,' said Mary.

'Carole has made a very good drawing of the man who attacked her. The sheriff should be able to identify him,' said Rufus.

Carole was staring at Ben. She knew

instinctively what his answer would be.

'No, I've got to go into Sula. Anyhow, if they find out that I'm still here they could come here looking for me. And that would put your life at risk.'

Mary tried another tack.

'Well, you stay here, my dear. There's no point in your going into Sula. You don't want to get mixed up in a gunfight.'

Carole's reply took them all by surprise. 'I'm going into Sula with Ben. I want to be there when he kills the bastards.'

Shortly afterwards Ben and Carole rode away from the house. They promised to come back to visit the couple.

'Do you think they will come back?' asked Rufus.

'If Ben manages to survive the shoot-out with the gang. By the way, I gave Carole one of the colonel's special guns. She might need it.'

'I know. I saw there was one missing from the display case. It was the small Italian gun.'

'That's right. The one that fires only one

bullet. At first she didn't want to take it. But I made her put it in the handbag I lent her.'

Ben and Carole were riding towards Sula in silence. Both were busy with their own thoughts.

Ben was concentrating on trying to figure what would happen when they reached Sula. There was no doubt in his mind that Collins and Menzies would be waiting for him somewhere. They would have worked out that he would follow them if they tried to run. The obvious possibility would be that they would escape over the border to Mexico – especially since Menzies was a Mexican. But Ben had spent a lot of time in the country – mostly chasing Apaches. He knew the governors in San Caldiz and Limos – two of the main towns. Menzies and Collins wouldn't be able to hide in those towns for long. No, everything pointed to the two outlaws waiting for him in Sula.

Carole, too, was thinking about what might happen when they reached Sula. Like

Ben, she had assumed there was going to be a shoot-out. As she had stated before they had left Mr Rawlinson's house, she wanted to be there. She was sure that Ben would be able to take one of them. After that it was in the lap of the gods. Her main hope was that the one Ben would kill would be Menzies. She knew she would never have peace of mind until she had seen his dead body.

They had reached the outskirts of Sula.

'We'll call at the livery stable, then I'll take you back to your hotel,' stated Ben. 'I'm going to book a room for myself there. I'll be around until you catch your train up north.'

Why couldn't she tell him that she wasn't going back to Boston? She glanced at his hard face. Maybe this wasn't the right time.

They had stabled the horses and were walking towards the hotel. It was a pleasant evening and many of the inhabitants were still on the sidewalk. The women were sporting colourful dresses and the men were out walking in their jeans and shirts, having left their jackets at home. Carole began to relax. Nothing tragic could happen on such a pleasant evening. She was tempted to take Ben's arm like many of the other strolling couples, but his stern expression deterred her.

Suddenly they heard the shout they were dreading.

'Daley!'

It came from the other side of the street. For Ben it was a case of *déjà vu*. He had no doubt that it was Collins's voice. He was also equally positive that the second he turned to face Collins he would be met by a hail of bullets from Collins and Menzies. The only reason he was still alive was that Collins wanted to see his face before killing him. The outlaw wanted to see the fear on his face before he sent him to meet his maker.

It took Ben several hundredweights of willpower not to turn to face the outlaws.

'Daley, I'm calling you.' This time the shout was full of impatience.

Ben knew that he had only a few seconds to live. Fortunately Carole was on the inside of the sidewalk and maybe she might have a chance of escape.

'When the shooting starts, get down on the sidewalk,' he hissed.

At that moment fate stepped in. It took the form of a cart that was carrying fruit and vegetables – probably from the market which had not long closed. It came along the road and for a few seconds it passed between the outlaws and Ben, obscuring their vision.

When the cart had passed it took the outlaws a second to realize that their two intended victims weren't where they had originally been. In fact they were lying on the sidewalk. In that second Ben shot Collins in the heart. Even as he shot the outlaw Ben realized he wouldn't have time to turn his gun on Menzies.

Then a strange thing happened. Menzies was about to finish off Daley once and for all when he noticed that the bitch he had attempted to rape also had a gun. But it was almost a toy gun. He ignored it and swung his own gun to cover Daley. He realized his mistake when he felt a sharp sting in his arm. It was enough to put him off his shot.

Ben's shot again found its target.

'I put him off!' exclaimed Carole excitedly. 'I put him off his aim.'

Ben got to his feet. He pulled Carole up.

'You did well, partner,' he agreed.

'Partner? What's this about partner?' There was more than a measure of ice in her tone.

Ben stared at her for a long time. At last he said:

'You did well, wife-to-be.'

'That's better.' Carole stood on tiptoe and kissed him.

An elderly gentleman who was passing remarked:

'I don't know what the world is coming to today. Kissing like this on the sidewalk.'

Ben and Carole ignored him.

The publishers hope that this book has given you enjoyable reading. Large Print Books are especially designed to be as easy to see and hold as possible. If you wish a complete list of our books please ask at your local library or write directly to:

Dales Large Print Books
Magna House, Long Preston,
Skipton, North Yorkshire.
BD23 4ND

This Large Print Book, for people
who cannot read normal print,
is published under the auspices of
THE ULVERSCROFT FOUNDATION

... we hope you have enjoyed this book.
Please think for a moment about those
who have worse eyesight than you ...
and are unable to even read or enjoy
Large Print without great difficulty.

You can help them by sending a
donation, large or small, to:

**The Ulverscroft Foundation,
1, The Green, Bradgate Road,
Anstey, Leicestershire, LE7 7FU,
England.**
or request a copy of our brochure for
more details.

The Foundation will use all donations
to assist those people who are visually
impaired and need special attention
with medical research, diagnosis
and treatment.

Thank you very much for your help.